CABS, CAMERAS, AND CATASTROPHES

Books by Wendy Lee Nentwig
from Bethany House Publishers

———— ❖ ————

*Departures**

Unmistakably Cooper Ellis

1. *Tripping Over Skyscrapers*
2. *Moonstruck in Manhattan*
3. *Subway Tokens in the Sand*
4. *Cabs, Cameras, and Catastrophes*

*with Robin Jones Gunn

UNMISTAKABLY 4 COOPER ELLIS

CABS, CAMERAS, AND CATASTROPHES

WENDY LEE NENTWIG

BETHANY HOUSE PUBLISHERS
MINNEAPOLIS, MINNESOTA 55438

Cabs, Cameras, and Catastrophes
Copyright © 2000
Wendy Lee Nentwig

Cover illustration by William Graf
Cover design by Lookout Design Group, Inc.

Published by Bethany House Publishers
A Ministry of Bethany Fellowship International
11400 Hampshire Avenue South
Minneapolis, Minnesota 55438
www.bethanyhouse.com

Printed in the United States of America by
Bethany Press International, Minneapolis, Minnesota 55438

Library of Congress Cataloging-in-Publication Data

Nentwig, Wendy Lee.
    Cabs, cameras, and catastrophes / by Wendy Lee Nentwig.
       p.   cm. — (Unmistakably Cooper Ellis ; 4)
    Summary: Sixteen-year-old Cooper regrets her decision to break up with Jason and jeopardizes her modeling career after sticking to her Christian beliefs during a risky photo shoot.
    ISBN 0–7642–2068–3 (pbk.)
    [1. High schools—Fiction. 2. Schools—Fiction. 3. Models (Persons)—Fiction. 4. New York (N.Y.)—Fiction. 5. Christian life—Fiction.] I. Title.
PZ7.N437746 Cab   2000   CIP
[Fic]—dc21   00–008334

For my dad, Loren,
who isn't sure I remember any of the good stuff,
but I do.
Someday I'll write about
the camping trips along the coast,
the games of Go Fish and War,
the Sunday afternoons watching *Wide World of Sports*,
that first skateboard you made me by hand,
and the rides in the back of your pickup truck
on warm summer nights.
Until then, know that they're not forgotten,
just tucked away for safekeeping,
and I pull them out to make me smile
more often than you'd think.

WENDY LEE NENTWIG is a graduate of Biola University and spent her college years studying journalism before launching into a diverse magazine career, including stints with *Virtue* and *Seventeen*. In addition to her journalistic accomplishments, Wendy Lee has worked extensively with teens, both overseas and at home, and has published two other young adult novels, *Freshman Blues* and *Spring Break*. A born traveler, Wendy Lee currently calls Nashville home, where she is Editor at Large of *CCM* magazine.

COOPER ELLIS rounded the corner and pushed through the throngs of Hudson High students brimming with end-of-the-day excitement. Their enthusiasm didn't seem to be contagious, though. It had been a horrible day, and all Cooper wanted to do was find Alex and get out of there. Of course, nothing in her life was ever that easy, which is why it wasn't until she was only a few feet from her friend's locker that she noticed he was standing there with Josh. Josh—who she had broken up with barely three weeks ago. Josh—who had been all but ignoring her since then. Josh—who she really, really missed.

Panicking, Cooper tried to blend back into the crowd and escape, but it was too late.

"Hey, Cooper!" Alex called, gesturing her over.

"Hi," she replied a little weakly as she came up beside him.

Josh didn't even bother to speak. Instead, he merely nodded his head in recognition of her presence, which, she noted bitterly, was only one tiny gesture away from ignoring her completely. The only reason he didn't do that, Cooper was certain, was because he was too polite. She wasn't about to let him know his coldness bothered her, though, so she began occupying herself by concentrating intently on a loose thread on her backpack that needed immediate attention.

It was too much to hope that Alex would try to make the uncomfortable situation less so. Instead, he feigned innocence and asked, "So where were you going just now? You know my locker's still right here, the same place it's been for more than a year and a half, right?"

"I guess I didn't see you," Cooper shrugged. The words were barely out of her mouth before she was whispering a quick prayer of apology to God for the lie. She wanted to claim special circumstances, but she refrained. She knew a lie was a lie, and she vowed to work harder at not using them to get herself out of sticky situations, no matter how humiliating they had the potential to be. One more thing to add to the list.

Why does it seem like no matter how far I come, there's always still more to work on? she wondered. Before she could find an answer, Josh broke the silence.

"I guess I'd better get going. I have band practice in half an hour," he said. "I just wanted to let you know how discipleship was going, Alex."

Then before Cooper could say anything more or Alex could humiliate her further, Josh was gone, lost in the sea of students washing past them.

"See, he can't stand to be within five feet of me!" Cooper complained. "Even as he said he was leaving, he was sure to direct that comment only to you."

"You're exaggerating," Alex told her unsympathetically.

"But I'm not!" Cooper protested. "He's barely spoken to me in biology class since we broke up."

"That's sort of to be expected, isn't it?"

"Not when we're lab partners!"

"You've got a point there," Alex conceded. "You have to remember, though, *you* broke up with *him*."

"Only because he wanted to spend every single second of the day with me. I was feeling smothered!"

"Well, that's certainly not a problem anymore," Alex shot back. When Cooper didn't smile at his joke, though, he softened. "Are you sorry you broke up with him?" he asked.

"I'm sorry I broke up with *all* of him," Cooper clarified. "I just meant to break up with the Josh who was acting so clingy. I'd still like to be dating the Josh who was my friend and made me laugh and seemed to really like me, even in a lab coat and protective goggles with frog guts all over me."

"I don't think anyone likes you in a lab coat and protective goggles with frog guts all over you. He was just being nice."

"That's exactly what I mean!" Cooper cried. "He's just so nice! Or he used to be, anyway," she said wistfully.

"Why don't we go to Cuppa Joe and we can discuss this in greater detail over some cappuccino?" Alex suggested. "I know I'm not as good as Claire is at dispensing advice or listening patiently, but since she's otherwise engaged with Matt right now, I'd be happy to lend you my shoulder to cry on."

"That would be really nice," Cooper replied gratefully, then added, "You know, you can actually be pretty sweet sometimes. . . ."

As they headed away from school and out onto the busy

New York City streets, Alex stopped and turned to Cooper. "You know I meant that figuratively, right? I mean, you're not really going to cry, are you? I don't do tears very well. Besides, I don't want to get makeup all over my shirt. It's my favorite one."

". . . And sometimes you can be a total jerk!" Cooper finished, punching her friend playfully in the arm. Even as she was scolding him, though, she couldn't help but smile a little. Alex always seemed to know how to do that at just the right moment, and she enjoyed being able to take their comfortable friendship for granted again. It was one of the only good things to come out of her breakup with Josh: Alex had stopped acting like a jealous boyfriend and had turned back into her old buddy.

Soon they had reached the cozy little coffeehouse near the Upper East Side apartment building she and Claire both called home, and Cooper pulled out her new cell phone to check in with Tara, her booker at Yakomina Models. She was relieved to find out she didn't have any appointments that afternoon, which meant she didn't have to rush off anywhere, but instead could hang out until dinnertime. She was booked for a job the next day, though, so she would have to remember to let her mom know.

Ever since a disastrous shoot in Connecticut about six weeks earlier, her mother had insisted on accompanying Cooper on any modeling jobs. Cooper had been so shaken up by the bad experience that she didn't argue. That was also why she had a cell phone now, for emergencies and so she could call her agency or her mom in case anything got out of hand. Still, it wasn't until the last few weeks that she felt somewhat relaxed again, and as a result, she was finally getting more work. After that she placed a second call to Ellis Hughes Interiors, the design shop her mother ran with Claire's mom. Now that she had checked in with half the free world, she could finally enjoy her coffee without worrying.

In the short time it took her to stow her phone and return her backpack to the beat-up green velvet couch where she and Alex sat, her mind had already switched gears and she was once again thinking about Josh.

"Maybe I should just tell him I made a mistake," Cooper suggested, tucking a few long, dark strands of hair behind her ear.

"But I thought you just said you didn't make a mistake. You don't want things to go back to the way they were before, do you?"

"I want *some* things to go back," Cooper said.

"So how do you tell Josh, 'I'd like to pick and choose just the stuff that I liked about us dating and have that back, please'?"

"I don't know. That's what you're supposed to be helping me figure out!"

Alex sipped his cappuccino thoughtfully as Cooper added another packet of sugar to hers, careful not to stir all the foam away.

"Okay, here's what I think you should do," Alex finally said when his cup was almost half empty. "Since you can't come right out and tell Josh you want at least part of him back, you'll just have to show him instead."

"What exactly did you have in mind?" a skeptical Cooper asked.

"It's simple. You don't have to have some big talk about what went wrong. Just let him know you're still interested. Talk to him about other things besides your relationship—or current lack of one."

"But he doesn't want to talk to me!" Cooper protested. Hadn't Alex been listening at all?

"He doesn't want to talk to you *now*. But if you're willing to swallow your pride and have a little patience, I'm sure he'll start talking to you again . . . eventually."

"I can't be too patient. There are only four more weeks of school left."

"That's plenty of time," Alex assured her.

"I'm glad you're so confident. I wish I shared your optimism."

"Stick with me and you'll be fine."

Cooper wanted to trust Alex. She had known him since junior high, and now here they were almost at the end of their sophomore year. But he had been really against her dating Josh in the beginning. Their other best friend, Claire, was convinced it was because Alex had a crush on Cooper, but that seemed impossible. And then, just as Cooper was ready to break it off, Alex suddenly seemed to warm to the idea of her and Josh as an item and he'd been supportive and back to his normal self ever since. Cooper wasn't sure what it all meant, but she decided to give Alex the benefit of the doubt.

"Okay, I'll make him talk to me if it's the last thing I do . . . this school year, anyway," Cooper announced. "I just feel so disconnected from his life, though. What was that he was saying about band practice and some discipleship thingie?"

"You didn't know? He joined that band John Bethea and his friends started."

"That's the same band he didn't want to join while we were dating because it meant time away from me!"

"I guess once he wasn't spending time with you anymore, he figured why not?"

"That's what is so frustrating about all of this. He's doing all the things now that I wanted him to do while we were together!" Cooper complained.

"Better late than never?" Alex ventured.

"Ha, ha, ha. Very funny," Cooper said, shooting Alex a withering look that let him know she thought he was anything but. She quickly refocused, though, and continued with her line of questioning. "That explains the band comment, but what was he saying about discipleship?"

"Since band practice interfered with our reading group, he asked me what I thought he should do. He was afraid that maybe he was putting God second behind the band."

"When did this happen?" Cooper interrupted. "And why didn't you tell me he wasn't coming to the reading group because of band practice? All this time I thought it was because he was avoiding me!"

"It was a private conversation. A friend came to me for advice," Alex said a bit self-righteously.

"I can't believe you choose now to develop some principles! We have private conversations and I come to you for advice, but that never stops you from using that information to humiliate me later. I can't believe you haven't mentioned this before now!"

"You never asked. Besides, you broke up with him. How

was I supposed to know you were still so interested in every little thing going on in his life?"

"Because you're one of my best friends, and I thought it would be clear to you that I still cared about Josh. After all, I didn't break up with him because I didn't like him anymore. I broke up with him because he was driving me crazy. That's completely different," Cooper explained and then punctuated the end of her speech with a long, exasperated breath.

"What can I say? I misunderstood. If you girls weren't so hard to figure out all the time, maybe I could keep up better," Alex said by way of defense. "Now, do you want me to finish my story or not?"

"Yes, but hurry. You're dragging this out on purpose."

"You're the one who keeps interrupting to argue with me."

"No, I . . ." Cooper began but cut herself off. If she was ever going to hear the rest of the information Alex had been holding back from her, she knew she'd better just quit while she was behind.

"Are you finished?" he asked.

"Yes," Cooper said meekly. "Go on."

"Weeeeell," Alex drawled, enjoying having his friend's undivided attention. "I told him he was only putting the reading group second, not God, and that there are dozens of other ways he can grow closer to God that will allow him to be in this band, too. So Josh talked to Pastor Redding, and he hooked him up with a college guy. I think he's a student at Columbia University or something, and they've been meeting together once a week. That's what he was telling me about when you showed up."

"Oh" was all Cooper could think to say.

"It seems like he's really growing. They've already read through the Gospels together, and this week Josh said he's supposed to set some personal and some spiritual goals to work on for the next month or so. It sounds kind of cool."

"That's great," Cooper said quietly. It wasn't that she didn't mean it or that she wasn't happy that Josh was so excited about his faith and growing in it. It was just sort of annoying that as soon as she broke up with him, everything in his life seemed to fall into place. As if she were somehow holding him back. How was she not supposed to take that personally?

COOPER COULDN'T WAIT to get to school the next morning. The perennially late riser was riding the elevator down three floors to Claire's apartment ten minutes earlier than what would have been termed "on time" and a full twenty minutes ahead of the time the girls usually managed to leave.

"Someone's a little eager to see a certain someone this morning, isn't she?" Claire teased after letting Cooper into her family's apartment, which was almost identical to the Ellises' upstairs except it wasn't as stark and spotless.

"It's so nice to finally have a plan," Cooper chirped. "I'm going to talk to Josh today whether he talks back to me or not."

Claire had been filled in by phone the night before so Cooper didn't need to rehash any of the details. Her best friend since babyhood agreed with Alex that the best thing to do was slowly but surely show Josh she still cared. Then maybe, eventually, they could start dating again, but without so much pressure.

"I think you're going to need that resolve, at least in the beginning," Claire warned. "But I'm sure he'll warm up to you again in time, and then maybe you can finally work things out."

"That's what I'm counting on," Cooper said as she watched Claire spray a little bit of hair spray on her shoulder-length, chocolate brown layers.

By the time Cooper headed for bio lab, though, her enthusiasm was waning a bit. Her stomach was making weird noises, and she was one big walking ball of nerves. She missed Josh and the easiness they used to share, and suddenly she doubted they would ever be able to recapture it.

Just as she was about to give up, however, she saw him. Josh was at his desk, waiting for class to start, his head bent over his binder and his longish brown hair falling down over his eyes. He was lost in concentration so he didn't even notice Cooper taking the seat next to him, but her determination was back and he wouldn't be able to avoid her for long.

"So how was band practice?" Cooper asked as if things had never changed and they were still talking on the phone every night and eating lunch together every day.

"Hmm?" was all Josh said by way of response.

But Cooper refused to be put off any longer. She repeated her question, willing her voice to sound even more casual than the first time.

"Oh, um . . . fine," Josh finally answered. He seemed as nervous as she did, which she hoped was a good sign.

"I didn't know you had decided to go ahead and do that after all. That's really great," Cooper continued, unwilling to allow the conversation to lose momentum now that it was started.

"Yeah, it's been good," Josh replied.

Before she could think of anything else to say, Mr. Robbins appeared and class began. Cooper was content, though. The ice had been broken and Josh hadn't completely blown her off. And she was feeling hopeful that things would only get better.

The next few days followed the same pattern. Cooper made the first gesture, and Josh responded positively, if a bit hesitantly, before class started and the interaction was over. But Friday was a lab day, and Cooper had high hopes for making some real progress. There were several dissection stations set up, and each team of lab partners had to stop at each station and come up with answers to the preprinted questions they'd been given. An entire class period of uninterrupted time with Josh!

Cooper had her work sheet and pencil and was standing eagerly by Josh's desk while most of the other students were still fishing in their backpacks, wasting time.

"Are you ready?" Cooper asked with more enthusiasm than she thought she would ever be able to muster for a lab assignment, especially one that involved looking at the insides of a dead cat.

"I guess we might as well get started," Josh conceded. He obviously wasn't sharing Cooper's excitement, but she hoped she'd be able to change that as the hour progressed.

Josh did eventually warm up to her a bit. Cooper helped facilitate that by reminding him of their first lab together when she had accidentally thrown their frog on the floor and making little jokes as they moved from lab station to lab station. She even had him laughing at one point, which gave her the encouragement she needed to ask him to join them

21

for lunch, something he hadn't done since the breakup.

"So, Josh, if you're not, um . . . doing, well, anything else, uh . . ." Cooper was still choking out the invitation when Micah, Mr. Robbins' teaching assistant, appeared at her side and casually draped his arm over her shoulder. He was a senior, and Cooper had watched the dark-haired athlete with interest since her freshman year. He'd been her first crush at Hudson High, and he had been the only thing that made biology class endurable before she got to know Josh. Now she hadn't thought of Micah in ages, but apparently he'd been thinking of her.

"I saw your picture in one of my sister's magazines last night," Micah began. "You looked really great."

"Oh, thanks," Cooper replied. It always made her feel a little uncomfortable when people commented on the modeling she did, especially people who hadn't seemed to have anything to say to her before she signed with Yakomina Models.

"Where was that at, anyway? You looked like you were on a farm or something. Do they pay to fly you first class to those places? If they do, I'd only take jobs that were shot in Jamaica or the Bahamas or something."

"We didn't have to fly anywhere. We were just in Connecticut," Cooper explained wearily. She had waited almost two years for Micah to talk to her, and she couldn't believe that when he did, this was what he picked to talk about. Not to mention he was messing up her plans with Josh. When Micah finally realized Cooper wasn't going to offer any more information about her fledgling modeling career, he put her out of her misery.

"I guess I'd better get back to work or Mr. Robbins will fire me. Then I'll have to take a real class that requires me to actually do something, and we wouldn't want that, now, would we?" Micah said before bestowing on Cooper one of his blinding smiles and walking back over to the teacher's desk.

It took Cooper a few minutes to recover from the odd encounter and to sort out her feelings. She couldn't believe that she had spent all that time dreaming about Micah, and now when he finally was talking to her, she had absolutely no feelings for him at all. Instead, it was Josh she wanted and she could barely get him to speak to her. Maybe if they ate lunch together, though, that would change. With that thought, Cooper began reissuing her invitation, with less stuttering and more determination this time. She wasn't even finished, though, before Josh was shaking his head to nonverbally turn her down.

When he finally did speak, all he offered was "I've got plans today," leaving Cooper to wonder what sort of plans and if maybe it was just his polite way of letting her down easy. Still, she decided to give him the benefit of the doubt.

"Maybe some other time, then," she suggested before smiling weakly.

"Maybe," he repeated with a shrug before walking off to turn in his assignment, leaving Cooper behind.

Josh's noncommittal response did nothing to boost Cooper's sagging self-esteem, and when the bell finally rang, she shuffled slowly down the hallway, not caring if she ever arrived at the cafeteria. Unfortunately, her friends weren't quite so patient.

"Where have you been?" Alex shouted over the noise of the other students as soon as Cooper came into view. "We've been waiting practically forever!"

Claire's question was asked silently, her raised eyebrow doing her talking for her.

"Forever's a bit of an exaggeration" was Cooper's only explanation. Then she collected her friends' quarters and took her place at the end of the Coke machine line. She was grateful for the time alone with her thoughts. She really wanted to believe that Josh had other plans and wasn't just using that as a convenient excuse to continue avoiding her, but she couldn't help feeling a little insecure. She was still puzzling through their earlier exchange when she heard a familiar-sounding song calling to her from the enclosed courtyard where she and her friends always ate.

Cradling the three cold cans in one arm and her Partridge Family lunch box in the other, Cooper made her way over to where Claire and Alex were, all the while still trying to place the song. Every Friday there were free concerts in the court-yard's mini-amphitheater, and any students—regardless of talent—were allowed to sign up for their turn. Sometimes the results were predictably disastrous, but at other times the music was actually pretty good. Today's performance fell in the latter category, so as Cooper distributed drinks to her friends, she craned her neck to try to see who was respon-sible for the soft folk-inspired sounds that were currently sur-rounding her.

With her arms still full, Cooper began to crouch next to Claire. She was almost sitting down when it all finally regis-tered. Cooper recognized the black retro shirt, worn khakis, and heavy work boots the guitar player was wearing as the same thing Josh had on just fifteen minutes earlier in biology class. She uttered a barely audible "Oh," and her lips were still forming that circle when her feet went out from under her, quickly closing the gap that still existed between herself and the ground. The rather ungraceful, sudden landing sent cans and her lunch flying. The old metal lunch box landed painfully on her shin before popping open and showering Cooper with cold pasta salad and yogurt. Her carrots were the only item that remained intact.

After a few seconds of stunned silence from her friends, Alex finally chimed in with, "I guess you noticed Josh's band is playing today, huh?"

Before Cooper could reply, Claire said, "I think she picked up on that, Alex," then grabbed their obnoxious friend's napkin and her own to help clean up.

"I keep thinking I'm going to grow out of this clumsy phase," Cooper confessed, dabbing at the pesto sauce on her pants.

"At least you're wearing black. It could have been worse," Claire consoled.

"Not that much worse," Cooper pointed out, her eyes not meeting Claire's but instead focusing on Josh in the distance. At least she had finally placed the song. It was from a CD of some little indie band Josh had loaned her a few months back. That's why she felt weirdly nostalgic when she heard it again.

As the music washed over her, Cooper allowed herself to wallow in self-pity. She stared at the greasy stain on her black pants and wondered for the millionth time why everything had to be so difficult.

I broke up with Josh because dating him was making me miserable, but now not *dating him is making me miserable,* Cooper thought to herself. *And he acted so hurt when I ended things, but he seems to be moving on just fine,* she continued while crinkling her forehead in thought and frowning at her inner monologue.

"Don't hurt yourself thinking too hard," Alex teased, interrupting Cooper's thoughts.

"It's just that maybe I won't be able to win Josh back after all," Cooper admitted to her friends. "I mean, I can't even stand the way that sounds—win him back—like he's some sort of prize you get at a carnival for shooting water in a clown's mouth or something. Ugh!"

"We know you don't mean it like that," Claire interjected loyally, nudging Alex as she did so.

"Oh, um, right," Alex added. The fact that his mouth was full of potato chips muffled his declaration, though, making him sound less than enthusiastic.

"It's just that I never thought I was one of those girls who only liked guys she couldn't have and then dropped them once she got them," Cooper lamented.

"You're not," Claire assured her.

"But how do you know? Maybe I am and this is just the first time you're seeing it. After all, I was so sure breaking up with Josh was the right thing to do, and now the second he moves on with his life, I decide I can't live without him."

"I don't think that proves anything except that you miss someone you thought was a good friend and maybe more,"

Claire said, continuing to act as interpreter for each of Cooper's statements.

Cooper had a harder time letting herself off the hook.

"How do you explain this, then?" she challenged Claire. "In biology today, Micah actually attempted to carry on a conversation with me, and I couldn't have been less interested. I think maybe I really am shallow and superficial, but you're just too good of friends to notice."

"Or maybe it's that Micah has the personality of a Pop-Tart, which is what I've been telling you for the last year and a half!" Claire said, a hint of exasperation in her voice. "I don't think it proves you're superficial. It proves you've finally come to your senses."

"Yeah, what's with all the sudden insecurity?" Alex added. "I think your lack of interest in Micah proves you're *not* shallow, if it proves anything."

Cooper wanted to believe them, but as she stared at Josh off in the distance, she had to wonder. If she wasn't any of those things, what went wrong? And more importantly, how would she ever make it right again?

"ISN'T IT ABOUT TIME for the weekly Friday Night Film Festival to begin?" Mrs. Ellis asked her daughter, who was busy polishing off a bowl of Cap'n Crunch.

"Alex should be here soon, but Claire has other plans tonight," Cooper explained, trying not to sound too dejected. She hoped her mom would let it go at that, but she knew it was doubtful. Her mother always liked to have all the details and would keep asking questions until her curiosity was satisfied.

True to form, she started in again with, "Claire's missing video night? But this has been a standing date between the three of you since you started high school! I thought you could only miss if you were hospitalized or bedridden with a highly contagious disease, and even then you needed a note from your doctor!" her mother teased.

Cooper shrugged, knowing that would only lead to more questions, but she was still trying to work up the courage to give the full explanation she knew would be required.

"That doesn't sound like Claire at all," her mother

persisted. "Is something wrong? It doesn't have to do with her parents, does it?"

"What would it have to do with her parents?" Cooper asked, momentarily distracted from the real issue at hand. "They never have a problem with her coming over since she practically lives here anyway."

"Oh, I don't know," Mrs. Ellis replied. "I'm sure they wouldn't. I don't know why I even said that."

Cooper gave her mother a strange look. It seemed it was suddenly Mrs. Ellis's turn to be vague, but her daughter couldn't figure out why. It wasn't like her mom to say things for no reason. Was there something else behind Claire missing movie night? Just as Cooper was beginning to get a bit paranoid, her mother tried her best to change the subject.

"So why couldn't she come, dear?" Mrs. Ellis innocently asked, her eyebrows raised expectantly as she waited for an answer.

Cooper decided maybe she was making too much of her mom's simple statement. Surely if Claire were having some sort of problem, she would know about it. With that settled, Cooper gave her mom the explanation that she still assumed to be true.

"It's not really Claire's fault," she began. "Matt's parents had tickets to some Broadway play they couldn't use at the last minute so they gave them to him. Claire had actually told him to try to find someone else to take, but I told her that was just stupid. I mean, we're not babies anymore. We're all sixteen and we're not joined at the hip like in junior high. We each have our own separate lives, and things are going to come up from time to time. It doesn't means she's deserting us or that it will become a regular thing," Cooper continued, hoping that if she said the words with enough conviction they would suddenly become more true—or at least she'd believe they were.

"Well, that's very mature of you," her mother said, giving Cooper a sympathetic look that meant she had picked up on her daughter's apprehension behind her brave words.

Cooper really had meant it when she'd encouraged Claire to go with Matt. After all, this particular show had won a Tony Award for costume design, and with Claire planning to become a designer someday, it would be great for her to see the clothes in person instead of just studying pictures in some magazine layout. Still, Cooper couldn't help feeling a little sad at the way things were changing. She'd never been good at accepting that sort of thing. Her mother interrupted her melancholy thoughts before she could completely depress herself, though.

"You are aware that sugary cereal does not constitute a balanced meal?" Mrs. Ellis half questioned, half pointed out, the sympathy and concern of a moment ago gone from her voice.

"Of course I am," Cooper replied, waving her hand dismissively. "This is only my first course. I'm also heating up some caramel dip to have with one of these," she announced, holding out a shiny red apple for inspection as if she were the Wicked Witch and her mother were Snow White.

When her mother frowned but didn't actually voice her disapproval, Cooper added, "Not only is the fruit and vegetable group represented, but apples are chock full of fiber!

Now, do I know my Food Guide Pyramid or what? Aren't you just so proud?"

Her mother raised her hands as if in surrender and was still shaking her head when she left the room.

"I'm making pigs in a blanket, too, if that makes you feel any better," Cooper called out after her mom's retreating form. She knew it wouldn't, though. Her mother didn't believe hot dogs had any actual nutritional value. Of course, that didn't stop Cooper from heading into the kitchen to prepare her questionably nutritious snacks before Alex arrived.

She went to work on the hot dogs first, wrapping them carefully in the gooey crescent roll dough, then popping them in the oven. Afterward, she sliced several apples before nestling the plastic tub of caramel, steaming hot, in between them.

Just because there will only be two of us tonight doesn't mean I can't make it sort of festive, Cooper thought to herself. Then, as if to prove her point, she took the cellophane off of a bag of popcorn, put it in the microwave, and hit "start." It had just begun to pop unrhythmically when the doorbell rang.

"Hey, it's Video Boy!" Cooper said cheerfully when she opened the door and found Alex standing before her with a bag of tapes. She then waved her arm in a sweeping gesture and motioned her friend inside.

"Greetings and salutations," Alex replied, stepping over the threshold. "What's on the menu for tonight? It smells really good in here and I'm starved."

Alex was always starved, but Cooper politely refrained from pointing that out. He lived with just his dad and younger brother, and true to the bachelor stereotype, they ate a lot of frozen food and takeout. That was why Mrs. Ellis was always trying to feed him when he came over. Her mom had also been great about cooking for Josh, who was only too happy to escape his own parents' vegetarian dinners. Thinking of Josh made Cooper suddenly sad, but she tried her best to shake it.

"I was just about to check out the drink situation. C'mon, you can help me," she told Alex, hoping that if she busied herself with a task, thoughts of Josh would begin to fade from her mind. Who would have imagined one little video night could be so fraught with unpleasant memories?

As she stood in front of the fridge, Cooper willed the cold blast from the appliance to wake her up from her somber daydreams and bring her back to the present. After all, she had good friends—even if one of them was absent tonight—videos to watch, a roof over her head, and a refrigerator full of food. God had given her so much, and here she was moping around like a big, ungrateful baby. She resolved to change her attitude right then and there.

"I'm only seeing diet in here, but I know there's regular hidden somewhere," Cooper announced to her friend, determined to stay positive. As she dug around in the back of the fridge, moving jars of specialty mustard and pickles, lox for her father's bagels, the baby carrots her mother was always suggesting as a healthy snack alternative, and several plastic containers filled with foods Cooper didn't recognize, she found some more cans.

"Jackpot!" she cried, but as she pulled them out she realized they were root beer and her heart sunk down into her stomach. Not that she had anything against the beverage, but it was Josh's favorite. She had bought these particular cans to have on hand back when he was still part of her life. Now he'd never be coming over to drink them.

Just then the usually less-than-perceptive Alex seemed to miraculously pick up on his friend's distress. "What's up?" he said, coming to stand beside her in the shadow of the Frigidaire. Cooper showed him one of the cans and he seemed to immediately understand.

"Do you want to pour them down the sink?" Alex asked. "Or we could always blow off video night and go do something else, something really loud that won't allow you any time to think about Josh."

"No, that's okay," Cooper replied. "It's just root beer. So let's pop open a few cans and start the first movie," she finished bravely. "By the way, what did you get?"

"Well, funny you should ask," Alex said, beginning to squirm a bit.

"You didn't get some slasher flick, did you? You know the rules against blood," Cooper reminded. "Just because Claire's not here, don't think you're going to get me to watch that garbage with you."

"Believe me, there's no blood," Alex said.

"Then what's the problem?" Cooper asked, grabbing the bag before Alex had an opportunity to answer. It took only a quick glance at the titles for her to understand.

"Of all the nights for me to finally give in and rent 'girl' movies, and now all this mushy girl-gets-guy stuff is only going to make you miserable!" Alex lamented. "The one time I do something nice and look what happens. That's why I don't do it more often, you know."

"It's fine. Really," Cooper told him, suddenly the one in the role of cheerer-upper. "I'm sure they're good. And I've actually been wanting to see this one," she added, holding up a box with a guy on the cover holding a huge bouquet of flowers and smiling irresistibly.

"You're just saying that," Alex countered. "We don't have to watch them. I think there's a *Space Ghost Coast to Coast* marathon on the Cartoon Network. Maybe that would be better?"

"No. We're watching these," Cooper said firmly. "This is ridiculous. It's not like I'm some fragile little flower. I can watch other people find happiness without dissolving into a puddle of tears over my own disastrous love life." Then on a lighter note she added, "And besides, I know how much you're looking forward to them, and I couldn't possibly deprive you."

"That's very brave of you," Alex replied, his voice tinged with a bit of sarcasm. "Not many women would make that kind of sacrifice for the viewing pleasure of others. You are such a giver!"

Cooper threw a pillow at her friend before settling in on one end of the couch. It wasn't until the credits were rolling at the end of the second tape that they said more than "Pass the popcorn" or "Do you need something else to drink?" Cooper had been waiting to bring up the rather obvious theme running through both films. It hadn't been hard to realize that not only had Alex picked romances, but each had as its plot a relationship gone wrong, then the girl had gone to great lengths to win her guy back.

"These weren't by any chance supposed to give me ideas, were they?" Cooper asked suspiciously after she had hit the rewind button on the VCR.

"What are you talking about?"

"The not-so-subtle theme running through both films," Cooper replied.

"You noticed a theme?" Alex innocently asked. "I must have missed it."

Since Alex dissected movies while they were still watching them, Cooper had a hard time believing that, but she decided to play along. "So you didn't pick up on anything that maybe tied the two videos together?"

"They were both romances," Alex said, still playing dumb.

"They were both romances about women who'd lost the men they loved and you know it!" Cooper finally cried.

"Well, now that you mention it, they were. So did you pick up any pointers?"

"Hmm," Cooper replied, stroking her chin thoughtfully as she pretended to mull it over. "In that first one the main character traveled halfway across the world and then risked her life in a war zone to be reunited with the man she loved. In the second one, Olivia Newton-John totally changed who she was so John Travolta would accept her."

"But it's *Grease!*" Alex pointed out, raising his voice for emphasis. "It's a classic!"

"I understand that, but it still doesn't mean I'll be slipping on some spandex pants or taking up smoking any time soon," an exasperated Cooper explained. "Even if it meant getting Josh back."

CABS, CAMERAS, AND CATASTROPHES

"Well, if that's the way you feel . . ." Alex shrugged.

Cooper could tell, though, that he was trying to keep a straight face. In fact, the words were barely out of his mouth before he burst out laughing.

"Sometimes you are so *not* helpful," Cooper told him even as she laughed with him.

"And sometimes *you* are so demanding," Alex shot back. "That's why we could never date."

Cooper froze at the words. Alex had been acting so strange and jealous when she began dating Josh and then things returned to normal, but they'd never really talked about it. Until now, that is.

"So you're saying you wouldn't date me?" Cooper finally asked.

"No way," Alex said. "I used to think maybe, but you're too high-maintenance for me."

"Really? I'm high-maintenance?" Cooper asked, wondering why Alex's words hurt so much when she knew she didn't want to date him, either.

Alex's face was serious as he nodded in response. But then with his head still bobbing up and down, he said, "No, not really," and a grin spread across his face.

"Oooooh! You can be such a jerk sometimes!" Cooper cried, at the same time feeling secretly relieved.

"Wow!" Alex replied. "This Josh thing really has shaken your confidence, hasn't it?"

Cooper merely shrugged in response and chewed on her lower lip.

Alex shook his head in disbelief before telling her, "I can't believe I even have to say this out loud, but you are one of the easiest people in the world to be with. If I didn't feel so comfortable around you, I wouldn't spend hours with you during the week and then come over here every Friday night. Despite what you may think, I don't show up here just for the food. I could get that anywhere. It's that you're one of the only people I feel like I can completely be myself with. And I bet that's what made Josh want to spend every second with you, too."

Alex had barely finished his little speech before Cooper flung her arms around his neck and gave him a huge hug, which, of course, made him all uncomfortable.

"You don't have to get all mushy on me," Alex complained, his cheeks burning bright red. "Keep it up and I'll take it all back."

Cooper smiled at his empty threat, but she let him go. She didn't realize how much Josh's rejection of her had made her question herself. She'd even started to forget that she was the one who rejected him first. If she felt this bad when the breakup was her idea, he must feel a million times worse. Maybe he just wasn't showing it. *If that's the case, I'll just have to double my efforts to win him back*, Cooper thought. *And I won't stop until I do!*

"REMEMBER ... I HAVE A SHOOT ... after school," a groggy Cooper half whispered, half groaned on Monday morning. She was perched precariously on the kitchen counter, one foot dangling down, as she picked at a strawberry bagel and communicated only what she needed to with as few words as humanly possible.

"I've got it written down in my book. I'll meet you on the corner of Hudson and Spring Streets at 3:00 sharp," her mother crisply announced. "Now, you'd better go get ready for school. You don't always have to be racing in just as the last bell rings, you know."

Cooper wanted to protest that she wasn't always running in late, but not only was her mom annoyingly correct in her assessment of her daughter's near tardiness, Cooper also didn't think she could bring herself to expend the energy it would take to argue the point. Instead, she looked down at her baggy pajama pants and faded YMCA T-shirt, both wrinkled from sleep, then glanced at the clock and noticed that her first-period class was set to begin in less than an hour. Slowly, grudgingly, she made her way down the hall to the bathroom and turned on the shower, immediately filling the pale room with steam.

Why do mornings never seem to get any easier? Cooper asked herself as she rushed to get ready. *Why can't school start at a civilized hour like noon?*

"It's discrimination against those of us who aren't morning people," Cooper continued to complain as she and Claire walked briskly toward school. "I think we should petition the school board for more afternoon classes."

"Just two more years and then we'll be in college. You can fill your entire schedule with afternoon classes," Claire consoled.

Unfortunately, to Cooper two years seemed like an eternity. It might as well have been two thousand years! She sighed heavily before trudging on and was cheered up only slightly by the fact that they beat the first bell without running at all.

In biology Josh was friendly, but he still acted like a puppy whose nose had been swatted a few too many times. No matter how nice Cooper was to him or how many times she tried to reach out, he still remained hesitant at best.

Riding the number 9 subway downtown after school, her thoughts were still on Josh and how to turn things around for good. *At least I'm not obsessing about what could go wrong at the shoot,* Cooper thought happily as the train rumbled along underground. *It's good to know I'm making progress in some areas.*

Exiting the Canal Street station, Cooper was even more surprised to realize she didn't feel any apprehension at all about that afternoon's job. Even when she arrived at the building where the modeling shoot was to take place, the anxiety that had gripped her in the past was nowhere in sight. She had even arrived before her mother! Another bright spot in her day.

At one minute before 3:00, Mrs. Ellis came rushing up, out of breath and looking nothing like her usual composed self.

"I'm . . . so . . . sorry," she huffed, pausing between words to inhale deeply.

"Why? You're right on time," Cooper replied. That was just like her mother to apologize for not being earlier to something than she was.

"No, I'm not sorry about that," Mrs. Ellis corrected, regaining a bit of her composure. "I had a client call with an emergency situation while I was at lunch. She was frantic so my assistant told her I'd come handle it this afternoon, but she forgot to consult my calendar first."

"No biggie," Cooper said and meant it. "I think I'm finally ready to go it alone again. Really."

"You're not just saying that to make me feel better?" her mother queried, searching Cooper's eyes for some clue as to her daughter's true emotions.

"C'mon, this is me you're talking to. You know I wouldn't do that," Cooper answered. "But if you don't stop staring at me, I'm going to change my answer."

"Well, I'll at least ride up in the elevator with you and check things out. Then I can get back to Mrs. Page's penthouse and figure out how to fix her wallpapering disaster."

"Okay, if it will make you feel better. It's really not necessary, though. Honest. I can go up alone."

"I know, but it will make me feel better."

When they got off the elevator on the tenth floor, Cooper and her mother walked down a plain white hallway before entering a pretty generic-looking studio space. A quick glance around the room revealed painted brick walls, big windows draped in white sheets, folding chairs scattered haphazardly, and photography equipment littering the scuffed hardwood floor. Cooper quickly located the stylist, Jen, whom she recognized from their meeting the week before when she was hired for the job, and strode purposefully across the room to introduce herself.

"Hi, Cooper," said Jen, wiping her hand on her jeans before offering it to shake. With her hair pulled back and not a speck of makeup on, the woman running the shoot didn't seem like she could have been out of high school for long herself. "Ally's getting her hair done and Lindsay's in the makeup chair, so we won't be ready for you for a few more minutes."

"No problem," Cooper replied. "I've got some homework I can work on until then."

"Okay, sounds good."

After the brief exchange, Cooper hurried back to her mother's side to reassure her it was safe to leave. "See, everything's fine," Cooper insisted. "There's even a female photographer, so I don't think I have to worry about getting hit on."

"Oh, that makes me feel so much better," her mother groaned.

"You know what I mean. It's fine. And I have your number so I can call you if anything happens," Cooper pointed out. It was only when she saw her mom's eyes grow round that she added, "But it won't. Now, go before that client's wallpaper dries completely and you never get it off her walls."

"Thanks, sweetie," Mrs. Ellis said, giving her daughter a quick kiss on the cheek. "I'll see you at home later. Oh, and if I'm not there by seven, call and order something for you and your father for dinner."

"Don't worry. We know how to fend for ourselves."

Then just like that her mother was gone, with only the faint scent of her floral-based perfume to remind Cooper that she'd been there at all. It was funny, but being alone energized Cooper. It felt good to be confident again that she could handle whatever came her way. With that in mind, she reached into her backpack to grab her English notebook but found her hand resting on her little portable Bible instead. Experiencing a sudden change of heart, she pulled it out and unsnapped the leather cover before turning to the Psalms. She and Claire had made a pact to read one chapter every day that month, and she was too busy catching up on other schoolwork during homeroom to do her daily reading then. She didn't get very far before she was interrupted.

"Jen said to tell you the makeup artist is ready for you," said the girl who the stylist had indicated was Lindsay.

"Thanks," Cooper replied to the striking girl with a headful of light brown curls that fell halfway down her back. She then turned away to stow her Bible.

Before she could, though, Lindsay was asking, "What are you reading?"

"The Bible," Cooper answered, holding up the tiny volume even as she braced herself for the other model's response. It wasn't that she was ashamed of her faith, she'd just learned that not everyone thought carrying a Bible around in your backpack was as normal as she did.

"Are they making you read that in school?" Lindsay asked.

"No. Why would you think that?"

"I thought I heard you say you were doing homework."

"Ohhhhhh," Cooper said, finally understanding where the confusion had begun. "I was planning to work on an English composition I have due this week, but I guess the Psalms were just more interesting."

"I always liked the New Testament better myself. Things seem to move a lot faster. And Jesus telling off those Pharisees, that was cool."

Cooper was almost too surprised to speak. This wasn't the response she had expected at all. Lindsay was the first person in the modeling industry she'd met who didn't seem completely turned off by the merest mention of God. "So where do you go to church?" Cooper asked excitedly.

"I don't," Lindsay said casually. "I guess I'm still a member at our Baptist church back home in Nebraska, but I haven't been since I moved to New York City last year."

"Well, you're welcome to come with me sometime if you want," Cooper ventured. "I'm sure it can be hard to visit a new church where you don't know anyone."

"Oh no, it's not that," Lindsay said, waving her hand dismissively. "I just don't really see any reason to go anymore. I mean, that was okay when I was back home, but I'm doing fine here without it. My career's going great—I'm shooting a Calvin Klein campaign next week—I've got an amazing boyfriend, and I just bought my first apartment in Greenwich Village."

Cooper didn't know what to say. Especially since this was the first job in more than a month where she didn't have to have her mom hold her hand, her ex-boyfriend could barely look her in the eye these days, and she still had to get her parents' permission to nail something up on her bedroom wall. She couldn't even imagine what it would be like to have her very own apartment. Finally Cooper just blurted out the most innocent comment she could think of. "How do you find time for school?"

"I don't. I took the equivalency exam a few months ago because I kept missing class to go out on modeling jobs. I've been working nonstop ever since."

"And your parents are all right with that?"

"Not really. But since I'm making more money than they are and I'll be eighteen in a year, they really don't have much choice."

Cooper couldn't imagine any area of her life where her mother and father didn't still have quite a bit of choice. Before she could think of anything else to say, Cooper's name was called from across the room. She'd been so caught up in her conversation with Lindsay that she'd completely forgotten she had somewhere to be!

"Oh, I'd better go. I'm probably holding up the whole shoot!" Cooper cried.

"Okay, see ya when you get done," Lindsay calmly replied.

Even as she was hurrying across the room, Cooper couldn't help but notice that Lindsay seemed like the kind of girl who never got flustered or nervous or insecure. She couldn't even imagine what that must be like. Cooper also couldn't imagine how she could possibly convince someone whose life seemed so perfect that she needed God just as much as the homeless man she had noticed in front of the building when she and her mother came in. Still, Cooper knew it was true. But how could she prove that to Lindsay?

"SO HOW WAS WORK TODAY?" her dad asked when Cooper arrived home around 5:30, turning his daughter's usual question around on her.

"Surprisingly, gloriously uneventful," she replied, grinning.

"I can't tell you how glad I am to hear that. Your mother left me a message that you were on your own, and she sounded a bit nervous about it. I know she wouldn't have been able to forgive herself if something had happened."

"She worries too much," Cooper countered. "And besides, I think things are looking up. I haven't had any weird shoots in a while, and I even invited one of the other girls to church today. Of course, she turned me down, though."

"That's great, shorty," her dad said as he ruffled her hair playfully before adding, "I mean that you asked her, not that she turned you down."

"It was weird. She said she had gone to church back home, but now she doesn't need it. And as she rattled off the wonderful things happening in her life, I found I had a really hard time making a case for my side."

"Well, maybe that's where you went wrong," her dad gently pointed out. "You don't have to argue people over to your side. God's not a debate to be won."

"But how can I show someone who doesn't seem to need God for anything how wrong they are?"

"First, by not thinking of her views as wrong. You have to meet her where she's at. Be a friend to this girl and let her see Jesus in your life. Maybe one day when all the things she's filling her life with aren't enough, she'll come around."

"I don't know about that, but I guess it's the best I can do," Cooper shrugged.

"That's right. That's all any of us can do. Now, why don't we get some dinner? Mom's message also said she wasn't going to be home for a while longer."

"Thai food?" Cooper queried, raising a brow as she did so.

"Sounds good to me. Let's walk over and pick it up. It's such a nice night," Mr. Ellis suggested.

"I'm right behind you."

As Cooper slurped the spicy noodles in her pad thai and chomped into the juicy pieces of chicken and shrimp, she was still thinking of Lindsay. At least it felt good to not be obsessing over Josh for once.

For the rest of the evening she worked on her homework, washed a load of laundry so her favorite cargo skirt was clean for the next day, and watched an hour of *Nick at Nite*, all the while rehearsing how she would show Lindsay what was missing from her life the next time she saw her. Before bed, as she finished reading the chapter Lindsay had interrupted her from earlier, she began to feel hopeful that she would actually help this other model change her life. And it was with that happy thought that Cooper drifted off to sleep.

❋　　❋　　❋

It was amazing to Cooper how every class leading up to biology seemed to drag on for hours. But finally she found herself sitting next to Josh again, and Lindsay was far from her mind now. *He seems to be letting his hair grow,* Cooper noted, glancing sideways in what she hoped was a subtle way. *And his nails are all even and trimmed. Didn't they used to be more jagged when we were dating?*

"I said, did you finish the assignment without any problem?"

Cooper heard the question, but it couldn't have been meant for her. She turned her head the tiniest bit in Josh's direction, skepticism written across her face.

"Fine, you don't have to tell me if you don't want to," he finally said, turning back to look at his notebook.

"Wh-wha-what?" Cooper stammered. "I mean, were you ta-talking to me?"

"That would be the assumption, since I started out my sentence with the words, 'Hey, Cooper,' but it's fine if you don't want to talk," Josh said. Now he definitely seemed hurt or maybe even mad, which was the last thing Cooper wanted.

"Oh no!" Cooper cried, then tried to calm herself down before saying any more. She knew she was making a complete fool of herself, but this was the first time Josh had initiated a conversation since they broke up and she was caught off guard. She took a deep breath and chanted to herself, *You can do this, you can do this,* before trying to continue a bit more slowly.

"Sorry, I guess my mind was wandering and I didn't hear you. Yes, I did my homework," Cooper managed to get out without stumbling over any of the words or having her voice squeak embarrassingly. As proof of her statement, she pulled the stapled pages out of her binder to look over the answers she'd filled in.

"And you didn't have any problems with number five?" Josh continued.

"I don't remember, let me see," Cooper answered, paging through her assignment. She willed the indifferent expression on her face not to change, but inside her chest she felt a little weight suddenly pressing on her heart. *So Josh was only talking to me because he needed homework help,* she realized sadly. She tried to tell herself it was better than him not talking to her at all, but she found herself a hard one to convince. She was still just staring at her answer about the digestive system of a cat and realizing she had no idea if it was right when Josh spoke again.

"It was a really hard one. I had to look it up on the Internet and it took almost an hour. I think Mr. Robbins must have made a mistake including it since we never covered that in class."

Again Cooper fought to not let her face show what she was feeling, but this time her heart was doing cartwheels in her chest—no, it was doing triple flips!—at the realization that Josh wasn't looking for help but instead was actually having a conversation. It was all she could do not to flash

CABS, CAMERAS, AND CATASTROPHES

him the biggest smile imaginable, and she had to remind herself to breathe so she didn't pass out from the shock of this happy turn of events.

"Yeah, that was a hard one," Cooper finally replied. "I guess I should have tried the computer myself." She hoped he didn't think she was fishing for the answer, because as much as she could use the percentage points, she felt it would be cheating. She knew if the situation were reversed, she would have felt uncomfortable providing Josh with answers he didn't work for. She was merely trying to keep the conversation going, but what would she do if he offered? *How do I always get myself into these messes?*

Before she could worry too much more, Josh let her off the hook—and made her day.

"I know how you feel about doing your own work," Josh began, "so I won't tell you the answer, even though the question was unfair. But if you ever need any help, call me and I'll tell you what Web site I used. That way you'll still have to do the work yourself, but at least you'll be sure to get credit."

Cooper was almost too stunned to reply. Not only had Josh remembered how she felt about cheating, but he had also invited her to call him! This was what she had been waiting for for weeks! She floated through the rest of class and afterward worked up the courage to ask Josh again if he'd join her for lunch. She didn't even stutter as she issued the invitation.

"Wow, I'd love to," Josh began, "but I promised John I'd meet him and the other guys in the music room. We've been working on a new song and it's not quite right yet."

Cooper's disappointment was tempered by the fact that

Josh seemed genuinely disappointed to have to turn down her invitation. "Maybe some other time," she offered.

"Definitely," he agreed before hurrying off.

As she dissected the exchange with Claire and Alex over lunch, she got excited all over again. She wasn't sure what had made Josh change his mind about her, but it was clear, they all agreed, that he had. Even Matt said it looked encouraging. And as Cooper saw how he was gently holding Claire's hand and looking at her adoringly, she started to believe she could have that again, too.

As they walked home that afternoon, Cooper used her cell phone to call and check in with Tara at Yakomina Models to see if she had any appointments. There was no sense in getting all the way up to her apartment only to find out she should be on a number 9 train headed downtown.

The receptionist responded the way she always did, as if she had no idea who Cooper was even though she called there every afternoon.

"I'll see if she's available," she said doubtfully before putting Cooper on hold.

"At least I don't take it personally anymore," Cooper said to Claire, laughing as they walked down the street.

Before her friend could respond, a voice on the other end of the line blurted out, "So I hear you did a great job yesterday." Tara hadn't even waited for Cooper to say hello. She was such a typical New Yorker. No time for small talk, just get right to the point. It was a trait Cooper was growing to appreciate in her boss.

"I thought it went fine, but who'd you hear that from?" Cooper queried.

"They called this morning and said they might want you for another job in a few weeks."

"Great, keep me posted. Anything else?"

"Nothing this afternoon," Tara replied, but her voice was drowned out by the sound of a taxi beeping its horn just a few feet away from Cooper.

"Where are you?" Tara suddenly asked, having obviously heard the noise through the phone.

"I'm walking home from school."

"Well, you be sure to write down that appointment as soon as you get home."

"I will," Cooper promised before hanging up.

By the time she had stowed the phone safely in her backpack, she and Claire were in the lobby of their apartment building. It was only then that Cooper noticed that her best friend had seemed a little quieter than usual. "Hey, you want to come up for a little while?" Cooper asked. "We can go through my closet and you can put different outfits together for me, and I promise to wear whatever you pick out to school tomorrow."

It was a favorite game of her fashion-minded friend, but Claire only shook her head and said, "Maybe tomorrow."

As the elevator doors closed, Cooper wondered what could be wrong. Everything seemed fine between Claire and Matt at lunch, so maybe it had something to do with one of the classes she had after lunch or maybe something had happened on the way to her locker. Cooper made a mental note to talk to Claire later that night and see if she'd be more forthcoming.

To get her mind off of things until then, Cooper fixed herself a snack and settled down to do her homework. She had a paper to write for English class, some math problems to do, and another assignment for biology. She had to admit she was secretly hoping it would be a hard one so she could take Josh up on his offer and call him. To stay motivated enough to get the rest of the work done, she was saving her biology assignment for last.

It was amazing how well her little plan worked. By the time her parents arrived home, Cooper had finished all of her other homework and was just pulling out her biology book.

"Can you take a break and help me with dinner?" her mom asked.

Cooper was usually thrilled to have a reason to put off doing her homework, but this time she wished she could keep working. Instead, she sighed heavily before gathering up her books from the kitchen table and depositing them on her bed before reporting back for kitchen duty.

"So what are we having?"

"Stuffed pork chops," her mom answered, then added, "Can you get me the baking dish? No, not that one, the bigger one."

Stuffed pork chops were one of her dad's favorites, but Cooper also knew they took a while to prepare. Why couldn't they be having pizza or something else quick tonight of all nights? Still, she knew her protests would get her nowhere, so she resigned herself to spending nearly an hour in the kitchen and asked, "What's the special occasion?"

"There isn't one," her mother replied. "I just feel like I've been working so much lately, I wanted to make up for all the takeout you and your father have been eating."

If she really wanted to make up for it, she'd let me go work on my biology homework, Cooper said to herself. Instead, her mother handed her a potato peeler.

As she ran the kitchen utensil across potato after potato, Cooper imagined how the conversation with Josh might go. She would start with her homework question, and then they would naturally begin talking about other things, reminiscing about their near-disastrous first date, the job Josh had taken in order to afford the nice dinner they'd enjoyed, the ride through Central Park after the dance, their first kiss . . .

"Honey, I only need you to remove the skin, not whittle down the entire potato," her mother pointed out, interrupting Cooper's daydream.

Cooper looked down at the poor potato that was now the size of a single French fry. "Oh, um, sorry. I guess I'm a little distracted."

"Anything I can help with?" her mother asked.

"No. I just have some biology homework to finish and I was sort of thinking about that."

Mrs. Ellis then surprised her daughter by saying, "Well, why don't you go work on it. I can handle things here . . . besides, I want to make sure I have some potatoes left to mash."

Cooper smiled widely and gave her mom a quick kiss on the cheek before racing down the hall to her bedroom.

"Biology must have changed since I took it," her mother called after her. "It was never that exciting when I was in high school."

Cooper was already scanning the questions in search of one she couldn't answer, though, and didn't even hear her mom's little joke. As much as she wanted to call Josh, she knew she couldn't, in good conscience, tell him she needed help on a problem she knew the answer to because that would be like lying. Never in her life had she wanted so badly to not be able to complete an assignment.

And then she found it: the question she'd been looking for. It was number 12, a complex query about the muscular system of a pig, and she'd never been looking forward to a conversation about animal dissection so much. She lifted the phone from its perch on her bedside table and set it in front of her unmade bed. Then she lifted the receiver and stared at the number pad. She knew the number by heart but was suddenly afraid to dial it. Instead, she put the phone down fast, as if it were a hot coal that was burning her hand.

This is ridiculous, she finally told herself. *He said I could call him. He practically asked me to call. For all I know, he's waiting by the phone right now. I can do this. Just take deep breaths. It will be fine.*

After her little pep talk calmed her down, Cooper tried again. This time she managed to dial and waited anxiously through three rings. Then there was a voice on the other end, but she was surprised to find it belonged to a female. In all of her imagining, Josh had always answered.

"Hello?" the voice repeated, a hint of irritation creeping in.

"Um, hello. Is Josh there?" Cooper managed to choke out.

"Is this Caroline?" the voice asked.

"Uh, excuse me?"

"I'm sorry. Can I tell him who's calling?"

"It's Cooper . . . Ellis," Cooper said, feeling immediately

silly for adding her last name. As if Josh knew all sorts of Coopers.

"Oh, hi, dear. We haven't heard from you in a while," Mrs. Trobisch said, recognition in her voice at last.

"Hi," Cooper replied, not sure what else to say.

"Well, I'll try to track Josh down for you."

While Cooper waited, her mind was racing. Who was Caroline?

"Hello?" a voice on the other end of the line said, but again, it wasn't Josh's.

"Hello, is Josh there? This is Cooper," she repeated, feeling her nerve slipping away with every syllable she uttered.

"Hi, Cooper. This is Josh's dad. I was expecting a call so I thought maybe the phone was for me. Josh isn't here. He's out somewhere or other. He must not have told his mother."

"Oh. Well, can you tell him I called? I had a question about our biology homework."

"Sure, I'll give him the message."

"Thanks," Cooper replied before hanging up.

That certainly didn't go as planned, Cooper said to herself. *And who on earth is Caroline?*

COOPER SPENT WHAT SHE was sure was one of the longest nights of her life waiting for the phone to ring. It didn't help that the silence only provided her with uninterrupted time to wonder again and again who Caroline was. Maybe Josh had a new girlfriend and he really was only trying to be helpful with the offer of homework help. Cooper couldn't bear to think about that, so she tried to find something to occupy her mind.

She only managed to pick at her dinner, prompting all sorts of questions from her mom about her health and emotional state, and only after submitting to the dreaded forehead test and proving she wasn't the least bit feverish was she able to retreat to her room again. There she paged through a fashion magazine, barely even registering the fact that there was text on the pages until her eyes came to rest on an article titled "Winning Ways: How to get his attention—and keep it."

Cooper told herself it was ridiculous to read an article about how to get a guy. She couldn't trust advice from someone who had never even met her or Josh . . . and yet advice from those who *did* know them hadn't been much help so far. Cooper found herself paging through the list almost against her will.

"Make the first move" was the first tip and one Cooper mentally checked off her list. *I've definitely done that*, she told herself. *And I've made the second move and the third one, too*, she thought miserably. *Not that it's gotten me anywhere.*

"Dress like a girl" came next. *As opposed to what?* Cooper asked herself before peering down at her baggy overalls and T-shirt. *Well, I guess it couldn't hurt to try to look a little more feminine for a change*, she thought, plucking at the denim she practically lived in.

"Never let him know you're waiting by the phone" was point three. *He doesn't know I'm sitting here*, Cooper argued, justifying her actions to the glossy piece of paper the article was written on. That was all she could do, though. The idea of actually having an uninterrupted conversation with Josh after all this time meant she would wait by the phone for a week if she had to, a thought that made her anxious to get to the next point in the article so she could stop feeling as if she were a failure at the game of love.

"Make him jealous" was the final point in the article. The writer then went on to explain that if other guys wanted you, it would make you suddenly seem more appealing to the guy you wanted. As much as Cooper hated to admit it, she knew the convoluted logic made at least some sort of sense. Still, she hated the idea of playing games. Dressing a little nicer was one thing, but pretending to be interested in someone she wasn't was a completely different ball game. Not that

Cooper could do anything about it, since how other guys felt about her seemed out of her control. With that realization she tossed the magazine aside and it slid off her bed to the floor.

It was half past eight, and Cooper began to fear the phone wasn't going to ring. She glared at the loathsome instrument before picking it up to check for a dial tone. Of course, it was working properly. She then contemplated calling Claire, but what if her call waiting suddenly malfunctioned and Josh couldn't get through? She then thought about running downstairs to check on her best friend, but then she risked missing Josh's call altogether. No, she should stay by the phone. Claire would understand and they could talk in the morning on the way to school.

So that was how Cooper came to spend an entire evening doing nothing but unsuccessfully willing the phone to ring. By the time she got under the covers that night, she was mentally exhausted. It didn't help that in her dreams she saw Josh running along the beach with a beautiful girl. They were laughing and darting in and out of the waves, and when she playfully splashed some of the salty water in his direction, he cried, "Caroline! Stop it!" before picking her up and pretending he was going to drop her in the ocean. Their laughter was still echoing in Cooper's ears when she woke up the next morning.

"Well, what are you all dressed up for?" Claire asked as soon as she opened the door and found her friend there.

Cooper was wearing a flowing print skirt with some red embroidery around the hem and a pair of sandals Claire had helped her find in Chinatown. On top was a tank top with delicate lace trim under her softest, most feminine sweater.

Then she had pulled the sides of her hair back and twisted them in a loose knot before securing them with two red chopsticks. She had finished the look off with a touch more makeup than she usually wore and some of the perfume her mom had given her for Christmas.

"It's not too much, is it?" Cooper asked pleadingly, suddenly self-conscious and afraid she'd made a big mistake. *All those hours by the phone must have affected my judgment*, she worried.

"No, you look great," Claire assured her before Cooper's imagination could run away with itself any further. "I just figured there must be something special behind it."

With that little bit of prompting, Cooper spilled her guts about waiting by the phone, the magazine article, and her attempt to look more "like a girl."

"This is because of a magazine article?" Claire asked incredulously. "I thought you were smarter than that!"

"I know, I know, don't believe everything you read. But I was desperate!"

"Obviously," Claire replied. "Why didn't you just call me?"

Then Cooper felt even more foolish as she explained how she was unwilling to tie up her phone line even though they had call waiting. "I'm hopeless, aren't I?" she finally asked, not sure she wanted to hear the answer.

"No, you're just in love, which has a way of making you do things you wouldn't do otherwise. But if it's any consolation, you look really nice and I'm sure Josh will notice. When he does, though, just remember he also noticed you before when you weren't taking the advice of some silly magazine article."

"I will," Cooper agreed. "And it could be worse, so just be glad I didn't follow some of their other tips like trying to make him jealous."

At that, Claire rolled her eyes. The pair had arrived at school now, and Cooper realized she still hadn't found out what was bothering her friend. Fortunately, she seemed fine now, so Cooper decided to let it go, especially since the first bell had just rung.

"I'm sure Josh has a good excuse for not calling you back," Claire whispered to Cooper so no one at the lockers around them would hear. If it had been Alex, he would have waited until Cooper was halfway down the hall and then yelled it, causing her face to turn as red as the apple she had stowed in her lunch box.

"Thanks," Cooper whispered back, grateful for the encouragement *and* for her friend's tact. "I'll let you know how it goes at lunch."

"I'll expect nothing less than a full report."

With that, Cooper hurried off to her first-period class, where her teacher seemed to be speaking in slow motion. In fact, everything seemed in slow motion until she arrived at biology and saw Josh sitting at the desk next to hers, hunched over his notebook.

"Hey, Josh," Cooper said by way of greeting as she slid into her own seat. To her extreme disappointment, Josh didn't even look up. Instead, he merely grunted back a half greeting of his own. This was definitely not going as planned!

Just when Cooper was sure Josh was lost to her forever,

he turned his head in her direction and sniffed the air for a second before asking, "Is that new perfume?"

"Yes. I mean, no . . . I mean . . . it's not what I usually wear," Cooper stammered, her heart beginning to beat double time.

"Oh, I like the stuff that smells like fruit salad better," he said before turning back to the assignment he was looking over.

Cooper willed her face not to mirror how crushed she felt on the inside. *All this work and all he can do is tell me he doesn't like how I smell?* Cooper moaned internally. *And not a word about why he didn't call me back last night, either.* Cooper spent the rest of class pouting. She knew it was babyish, but she couldn't help it. She felt the rejection washing over her in waves, each one strong enough to knock her over, and then to have to sit next to Josh for fifty minutes on top of it all! That was too much to take.

Somehow Cooper managed to hand in her incomplete assignment—she had never managed to answer the question she called Josh about—and open her book so she could at least stare at the right page, but that was as far as she got. Halfway through class she thought she'd go crazy if she didn't get some air. But when she raised her hand to ask Mr. Robbins for the bathroom pass, he told her it was already checked out. She'd have to wait until the other student returned with it.

This is just great! Cooper complained to herself. *They're holding my bladder hostage!* Then just when she was sure it couldn't get any worse, Josh turned to her again. Perfect! Maybe he's going to tell me all about Caroline and how she wears just the right perfume and the right clothes and doesn't let stupid magazine articles mess up her love life.

Instead, the conversation took a decidedly positive turn. "Sorry I was so focused before," Josh began, "but I didn't get a chance to finish my homework last night so I was doing it before class."

"That's okay," Cooper managed to choke out.

"No, it's really not, but rehearsal went late and I forgot we had an assignment," Josh finished, misunderstanding her meaning. Cooper didn't mind, though. Her heart was soaring at the news that he had been with his band last night instead of Caroline, whoever she was. And that also explained why he hadn't called! Then it got even better.

"So are you eating with Claire and Alex today like usual?"

Cooper was trying to find just the right answer that would let Josh know she was dying to have him join them, but without sounding completely desperate. Before she could get the words out, though, Micah appeared before her desk holding the four-pack of toilet paper that served as Mr. Robbins' bathroom pass.

"Um, that's okay. I'll wait until after class," Cooper said, waving Micah away and turning her attention back to Josh.

Micah wasn't so easily brushed off, though.

"You're looking especially nice today, Ellis," he began, taking in her carefully chosen outfit and smiling at her with the self-assurance of someone convinced everything was done for his benefit, as if every girl at Hudson High lived only to impress Micah. His cockiness made Cooper wonder for the hundredth time what she ever saw in him, but she couldn't dwell on that now. There were more immediate issues to deal with.

Cooper wanted to quickly explain to Josh that it was what *he* thought that she was concerned with, but Micah just kept talking to her, oblivious to the cold reception he was getting.

"So what do you have planned for next Saturday night?" Micah asked, leaning over her desk to get even closer.

"Nothing, but it's still more than a week away. I'm sure I'll come up with something," Cooper answered before turning back to Josh. "Now, what were you saying about lunch?"

Before Josh could reply, Micah chimed in again. "Thanks to me you don't have to come up with something to do. I have two tickets to this off-Broadway show my brother's roommate is in," he announced, catching Cooper completely off guard. She could feel her eyes growing big as she began to comprehend exactly what had just happened. Then, while she was still trying to figure out how things had gone so horribly wrong, Mr. Robbins summoned Micah and there was no time to undo the damage. To make it worse, Micah turned to Cooper and over his shoulder called, "We can work out the details next week, Ellis. I'm looking forward to it."

One look at Josh told Cooper all she needed to know. Micah's little invitation more than negated any progress they had made in the past month, and they were right back to square one, only worse. Not only did she not have Josh, but she now had a date with Micah!

Why was it just when Cooper was always sure things couldn't get any worse, they did?

"YOU AGREED TO WHAT?" Claire and Alex cried in unison over lunch.

"Well, um, it's not like I actually agreed!" Cooper argued in vain. "And how was I supposed to know he was asking me out? It's not like I get asked out every day or anything. He caught me off guard."

"That's okay. I'm sure you three will make a beautiful couple, and you and Micah and his ego will live happily ever after."

Claire must have noticed the stricken look on her friend's face, for she suddenly said, "Alex, you're not helping, you know."

"Yeah," Cooper agreed. "If you really want to help me, figure out a way for me to get out of it."

"I'm sure if you just explain to him that you'd rather not . . ." Claire began.

"Or if you said you had to . . ." Alex chimed in.

"Or maybe if you just . . ." Claire tried again, but she was forced to let her thought trail off before it was even finished.

"See! It's not as easy as it seems, is it?" Cooper countered.

"I don't want to lie, and even to make other plans and then tell him I'm busy now seems dishonest. The alternative is to tell him I find the thought of spending an evening with him horrifying."

"I think you can word it a little more gently than that," Claire admonished. "I mean, even Micah has feelings—or at least I assume he does."

"Why do these things always happen to me?" Cooper groaned as she dipped a wheat cracker into a clear plastic container of sun-dried tomato hummus. "You'd think I wore a sign inviting these sorts of misunderstandings. And to make it worse, I really think Josh was about to say he'd join us for lunch, too."

"This doesn't mean he won't eat with us another day," Claire added, her voice filled with what sounded like forced optimism.

"Thanks," Cooper mumbled. She knew neither of her friends really believed that, but she preferred to let the statement go unchallenged for now. There would be plenty of time later to confront the sad truth.

It wasn't until the walk home after Alex had turned toward the subway station that Cooper finally asked Claire how she had been doing lately.

"I'm such a horrible friend! I've been so wrapped up in my own problems, I don't even know what's going on with you. Is everything all right these days?" Cooper queried.

"Well . . . not exactly, now that you ask."

It wasn't the answer Cooper had expected at all. She knew something had been on Claire's mind, but her friend was always the stable one, the one who solved other people's problems and never really seemed to have any substantial ones of her own. For her to have a problem she hadn't been able to solve on her own was a bit alarming.

"What is it? Why haven't you said anything before?"

"It's not really something I can talk about."

"Claire! You can't just tell me something's wrong and then not tell me what! How am I supposed to help?" Cooper complained, feeling helpless.

"That's just it. You can't help. There's nothing you can do to fix it. There's nothing I can do, either."

"But why? Is it something with Matt? Are you guys breaking up? And here I've been going on and on about Josh, and Matt just broke your heart! Why didn't you stop me?"

"Because Matt didn't break my heart," an exasperated-sounding Claire replied. "Matt and I are fine."

"Then is it something with school? Are you failing a class? If you are, I'm sure you can get a tutor. Or I'll help you. What subject is it?"

"It's not school" was all Claire said by way of an answer.

"Then what is it? Why won't you tell me so I can do something?"

"Because I've already told you, there's nothing you can do. And I can't give you any more details right now."

"Then how can I help?" Cooper asked for what felt like the hundredth time.

"Just be my friend," Claire replied simply. "Just be my friend."

The second time Claire said it she sounded as if the words took all the energy she had. This made Cooper even more worried than before, but instead of asking any more questions, she merely flung her arm over her friend's shoulder and said, "Always" before giving her a little squeeze.

They were silent the rest of the way home and even once inside until the elevator stopped at Claire's floor.

"Do you want to come upstairs and hang out for a while?" Cooper asked. "You can have complete control of the remote. I'll even watch *Pride and Prejudice* with you for the billionth time and not say anything when you forward to the scenes with Mr. Darcy in them."

Even with such wonderful enticements, though, Claire declined.

"Well, call me if you need anything," Cooper said before the elevator doors closed. "Really, I mean *any*thing."

"I will," Claire promised.

Once upstairs, Cooper called to check in with Tara. She found out she had been booked for an upcoming job and dutifully noted the appointment in her calendar. She then called her mom to let her know she had arrived home safe and sound. It was an old ritual that seemed unnecessary now, even babyish, but it was one she'd been unable to persuade her mother to give up. With those chores done, Cooper rummaged through the fridge in search of a snack, finally settling on fruit salad with some of her mom's sweet yogurt sauce on top. She dished it up and planted herself in front of the TV. She had homework to do, but after the horrible day she'd had, she felt she deserved a little relaxation first.

As Cooper watched cartoons, though, she found that her mind was wandering. She kept thinking of Josh, her upcoming date with Micah, and her best friend who was obviously upset about something. It wasn't fair that Claire, who was always there to help her, had a problem that Cooper couldn't help with. *Or is it that you just can't help in a way that would make you feel better?* asked a tiny voice in Cooper's head. Suddenly she felt convicted. It was true, part of what was bothering Cooper was that Claire wouldn't allow her to offer some useless advice and then feel better by doing so. She felt so helpless—in so many situations.

Unable to sit still any longer, Cooper wandered into her room. Her bed was unmade, as usual, and three discarded outfits were still where she had left them that morning. She added what she was wearing to the pile and slipped into her comfortable overalls and a T-shirt from Rod's Drive-In, a little diner she and Claire and Josh had visited during their spring break trip to the shore. As she secured the last overall buckle, she found herself thinking, *Now, that's better. Dressing like a girl only got me into trouble.*

Then her eye caught her Bible, open on her bedside table from her quick reading the night before, and Cooper scooped it up. Once she was comfortably situated on her bed with her legs folded, she deposited the heavy book in her lap and began reading where she had left off. She read several chapters and checked them off in the little "Read Through the Bible" pamphlet she had tucked away inside her Bible's front cover. She was a little behind for the year, but she was determined not to let that be an excuse to give up altogether. She was still reading more than she ever had, and going through the Old Testament in order was proving to be more interesting than she had expected. In fact, she found herself returning to one of her new favorite stories, that of Ruth and Naomi.

"Where you go I will go, and where you stay I will stay."
As she read the now-familiar passage from the first chapter of Ruth, Cooper prayed that God would allow her to be that kind of friend to Claire. She wanted to not just offer advice but to be there quietly when Claire didn't feel like she could explain what was wrong. It was something Cooper, who felt compelled to voice every feeling or emotion she ever had, especially had trouble with. But she was determined to work on it and be what Claire needed instead of what she wanted her friend to need.

Cooper was feeling much better by the time her parents came home, so much so that she even volunteered to help with dinner—again. She was busily spreading garlic butter on the bread before sticking it under the broiler when the phone rang.

"Can you get that?" her mother asked from where she was chopping the salad ingredients. She held up her hands with tomato juice dripping down them to show Cooper why she couldn't do the honors.

It turned out it was just Mrs. Hughes.

"Can she call you back?" Cooper suggested without even consulting her mom. "She's up to her elbows in salad junk."

"Actually, I really need to talk to her now. I can wait for her to get cleaned up." It was only then that Cooper heard the catch in Claire's mother's voice and realized the call was urgent.

"Is everything all right, Mrs. Hughes?"

It sounded like she started to say yes, but instead she just blurted out, "I'm sorry, Cooper, but can you please just get your mother?"

Before the words were even out, Cooper had returned to the kitchen. She covered the mouthpiece and whispered to her mom, "Mrs. Hughes is on the phone and she sounds really upset. She says she needs to talk to you right now."

Cooper caught sight of her reflection in the oven door and was surprised by the stricken look on her face. What was even more surprising to her was that her mother didn't seem startled by the urgent phone call. Her forehead was creased and her lips sort of pinched up, which happened when she was stressed, but it was obvious by her response she knew just what the phone call was about.

"Is something wrong at the shop?" Cooper persisted before passing the phone to her mom.

"The shop is fine," her mother replied distractedly. Then before Cooper could gather any more information, the phone—and her mother with it—disappeared down the hall.

While Cooper wondered what was going on in the apartment three floors below her own, she finished getting dinner ready. Fifteen minutes later, the salad was tossed, the garlic bread toasted to a nice light brown, the steaks grilled to near perfection, and the table set, but her mother still hadn't emerged from her bedroom. When Cooper could stand it no longer, she went into the living room looking for some input from her dad.

"Mom's still on the phone with Mrs. Hughes and dinner's getting cold. Should I go get her?" Cooper asked hopefully.

Instead, her dad suggested they go ahead and eat alone. Cooper started to protest, but something about the expression on her dad's face stopped her. They ate in near silence, as if they were mourning something, but Cooper didn't know what. She wanted to ask, but she knew she couldn't. For some reason, whatever was going on was not something anyone wanted to share with her at this moment, so she concentrated on her dinner, counting how many times she needed to chew each bite. Meat took fifteen, salad twelve, and bread a mere nine. She was just about to start guessing how much other foods would take—like her lunch, for instance—when her mother finally reappeared looking what could only be described as somber.

Cooper was dying to ask a million questions, but she sensed the timing was still all wrong. Instead, she only said, "We put your plate in the oven so your dinner would stay warm." Then she got up and rinsed her own dirty dishes and loaded them in the dishwasher. Usually she would leave them in the sink if it wasn't her turn to do dishes, but that somehow didn't seem right tonight.

Cooper was almost out of the room before her mom finally spoke.

"Claire's going to sleep here tonight, so you might want to straighten up your room a bit and put some clean sheets on your bed."

A sleep-over on a school night? And since when did she clean her room for Claire? Suddenly Cooper knew this was worse than she had even imagined, and without a word she retreated to her room and began straightening up.

All the questions she'd been wanting to ask faded away. She didn't want to know anything. Cooper wanted to travel back in time to the night before, or *any* other night, back to a time when life made sense and the only secrets parents kept from you had to do with Christmas presents or birthday surprises or other things that ended with everyone smiling and happy. Cooper already knew there was no way this was going to end happily, whatever it was. That thought made her feel way too grown-up and like a scared little kid at the same time—neither of which she wanted to be at the moment.

COOPER HADN'T EVEN HAD time to hang up her clothes before her best friend was standing in her bedroom doorway with her Asian-print overnight bag slung over her shoulder. It was the same one Claire had taken when the girls visited Cooper's aunt in Seattle the summer before, and the one she always brought along when she slept over. To Cooper, that bag had always seemed to signify the promise of fun times ahead—until now, that is. But there wasn't time to think about that, so Cooper attempted to push aside the fear she was feeling and forced the corners of her mouth to rise into what became a poor imitation of a smile. She knew her expression looked unnatural, but it was the best she could do.

"So, sleeping over on a school night, huh? Who would have ever thought Mom would go for that?" Cooper tried to joke, but her attempt at humor fell flat.

Instead of responding, Claire merely dropped her bag inside the doorway and plopped down heavily on the bed. That was something Cooper frequently did, but it was out of character for Claire, who was more of a "percher." She would perch precariously on the edge of a bed or chair, her back straight and her knees and ankles together like a graduate from one of those outdated charm schools.

"Do you want to watch some TV?" Cooper tried again, forcing her fake smile to stay put. It was awful feeling so awkward around her own best friend. What she really wanted to do was shout, "Will you please tell me what is going on?!" Of course, she knew she couldn't. Instead, she would have to wait for Claire to bring it up.

Fortunately—or maybe it was unfortunate, Cooper wasn't altogether sure—she didn't have to wait long.

"I think my parents are getting a divorce," Claire finally blurted out, her eyes brimming with tears as she did so.

"Oh wow! Are you sure?" was all Cooper could think to say. She was surprised she'd even managed to get those words out since she felt like someone had just hit her in the stomach and she couldn't catch her breath. Then she realized that if that's how *she* felt, Claire must be feeling a hundred times worse. Knowing that, she leaned over and put her arms around her best friend and hugged her for the longest time.

"It does seem really out of the blue, doesn't it?" Claire sniffled, her face still buried in Cooper's hair. "I mean, it's not like I thought they were ecstatically happy, but I had no idea they were thinking of breaking up. Aren't they supposed to fight a lot and scream and yell before they get to this point?"

"You would think so," Cooper agreed. "If it makes you feel any better, they always seemed okay to me, too." As she said the words, though, Cooper realized that she had never given the Hugheses' marriage much thought. They were always just together. And now, even as she was faced with that changing, she knew she couldn't imagine them any other way.

"It just isn't fair for them not to at least have given me some warning!" Claire continued.

"So you just found out in the past couple days?" Cooper asked. "I mean, this *is* what you couldn't tell me earlier, right?"

"The reason I couldn't tell you anything earlier is because I didn't really know what was wrong. Both of my parents have been really secretive the past few days and acting strange, but I kept hoping it was nothing. Then yesterday before school I found my mom in the kitchen crying. She didn't see me, but that's when I first realized this probably wasn't going to just go away."

"You could have talked to me about it," Cooper insisted.

"I didn't know what to say," Claire shrugged. "And you didn't see her sitting there looking so helpless. It was horrible. Besides, I thought if I talked about it, it would somehow make it real. I wasn't ready for that."

"So when did they actually tell you what's going on?"

"They waited until my dad got home tonight, and then they said they needed to talk to me about something and would I please turn off the TV. I prayed really hard that I would be wrong and instead they would just want to discuss where we should go for vacation this summer or something. I even found myself hoping that the problem wasn't with them, but that maybe some distant relative had suddenly contracted a serious disease. Isn't that awful? But of course it was about them."

"What exactly did they say?" Cooper gently prodded. She

was still hoping that maybe there had been some sort of mis-understanding and they were only *considering* divorce but hadn't really decided anything yet. Maybe they would go to marriage counseling for a while or take a second honeymoon trip to the Poconos and everything would be fine again.

"They started out by saying a bunch of junk about how this has nothing to do with me and they both love me very much—and then they dropped the bomb. They haven't been happy together for a while. They've grown apart. They don't want to start resenting each other, and they're afraid if they stay together just for my sake, we'll all end up miserable," Claire finished, her voice remaining monotone throughout, which made her sound as if she'd been reading from a list rather than recounting the demise of her parents' eighteen-year marriage. The tears threatening to fall from the corners of her eyes betrayed how emotionally draining the retelling was for her, though.

"So do they think this is going to make you less miser-able?"

"You know, I actually think they do," Claire sniffed. "It's like they're just not thinking straight or something. None of the things they're saying seem to make sense except to them, as if they've fallen into some parallel universe where wrong is right and up is down and divorce is good and marriage is bad."

"Maybe after they have some time to think it over, they'll change their minds," Cooper suggested hopefully.

Claire was skeptical, though. "They seemed pretty deter-mined to go ahead and at least separate for now. And if they're not even living in the same apartment, I can't imagine they're going to be able to talk enough to work things out. After all, if they grew apart living together, putting a good chunk of Manhattan between them isn't going to make them suddenly feel closer."

Then just when it seemed it couldn't get any worse, a horrible thought occurred to Cooper. "You're not going to have to move, are you?" She felt awful for even asking it, for worrying about how this whole thing was going to affect her when Claire would obviously feel the impact so much more, but she couldn't help it. They had lived in the same apartment building for almost six years, and before that their families had only been blocks apart. She didn't know what she'd do if Claire weren't three floors down. Before her imagination could get any further, her fears were put to rest.

"I'm not going anywhere—for now. I think my dad is going to try to find a furnished apartment to sublet until they figure out exactly what they want to do. So my mom and I are staying put. Who knows what will happen tomorrow, though."

"It's not much, but it's something. Right?" Cooper asked. She didn't want to push, but Cooper was also eager for any good news in the middle of all the bad.

"Right," Claire agreed. "I don't know what I'd do if on top of everything else I had to move."

"What are your parents doing now? I mean, why are you staying over?" Cooper asked, then hastily added, "Not that I don't want you here or anything!"

"It's fine," Claire assured her. "I know what you mean. And the reason I'm up here is that my parents are talking about a bunch of financial stuff and also when my dad's going to . . ." Cooper's best friend couldn't finish her sentence, though, and the words were just left dangling in midair as she started to quietly cry.

"I'm so sorry" was all Cooper could think to say as she handed Claire a box of Kleenex she had managed to unearth from a pile of stuff on her disorganized desk. She knew the words did no real good, but it gave her something to say, so she repeated the phrase several more times as she patted her friend's back helplessly.

"It's just not supposed to be this way!" Claire finally said when she was able to speak again. "They made a vow in church! They can't just change their minds like this!"

Cooper was taken aback by her usually calm friend's quick change from tears to tirades. Not that she could blame her for feeling angry about what was happening to her family. It was just that for the millionth time that night, Cooper had no idea how to respond.

"Before I left, I asked them if they were going to try to work things out at all, and they both just sort of looked at the ground. It's like they just want it to be over, like they can't wait to throw out almost two decades of marriage!"

"Maybe when they have some time to think, they'll see what a mistake they're making," Cooper suggested.

"I wish I could believe that," Claire replied sadly.

Cooper couldn't stand to see her friend looking so heartbroken, which was the only explanation she could give for the words that came out of her mouth next: "We'll just have to *make* them see that, then, won't we? We'll come up with a plan to get your parents back together!"

"What kind of plan?" Claire asked, her voice a mixture of hope and skepticism.

"A foolproof one" was all Cooper said by way of explanation. "Now, grab my computer and get that notebook there and let's get to work. We have a marriage to save."

It was nearly midnight when Mrs. Ellis knocked gently at the door.

"How are you girls doing in here?" she asked as she poked her head inside Cooper's room. Her face registered surprise when she took in the books and notebooks spread across the bed and the way the girls were so focused on what they were doing.

"We're fine," Claire answered, and for the first time that night she sounded like she really was. Cooper even managed to flash her mom a smile.

"Are you working on a project for school?" Mrs. Ellis asked next.

"Something like that," Cooper said, not offering any further details. She could tell by the look on her mom's face that she was completely confused and wanted to come right out and ask what was going on, but Mrs. Ellis knew that wouldn't be polite in light of what Claire had already been through that night. Cooper whispered up a quick prayer of thanks for her mother's impeccable manners and then said, "I guess we should get to bed, huh?"

Now her mother would *know* something was up—Cooper never voluntarily went to sleep before being told. But again she held her tongue. Instead, she gave each girl a questioning look and a kiss on the cheek before saying goodnight and closing the door behind her.

As soon as she was gone, Cooper and Claire shared the knowing look of two co-conspirators. Content with the knowledge that they were off to a good start and that their plan hadn't been discovered, they cleared off Cooper's double bed and made sure the notes from their night's work were safely stowed out of sight.

It was only after they were in bed with the lights out that the mood turned somber again.

"Cooper?" Claire asked through the darkness.

Cooper's eyes hadn't adjusted to the dark yet. She couldn't make out her friend's face a few feet away, but she could detect the faint scent of cinnamon from the toothpaste Claire had just used.

"Yeah?" Cooper answered.

"I'm really scared."

"I know. So am I."

BY LUNCHTIME THE FOLLOWING DAY, the girls had brought Alex up to speed. Since his own parents had been divorced for almost as long as he could remember, the news didn't seem to surprise him quite as much as it had the girls, but still he was uncharacteristically sensitive and genuinely concerned about Claire. When it came to the plan, though, he was a little less supportive.

"You know this isn't like in *The Parent Trap*," Alex cautioned. "That movie was completely unrealistic—both the original *and* the remake. And while I know you two think of yourselves as practically sisters, you are not twins separated at birth. Also, I can't imagine you getting your parents to go off on some camping trip, even if it would save their marriage."

"We weren't going to try to convince them to go camping," Cooper told him. "That would be ridiculous. There are other things we can do, though."

"Like what?" Alex asked, his voiced tinged with skepticism.

"We found some interesting information on the Web last night," Claire began.

"And we have a list of books we're going to look through at Barnes and Noble after school today and make some notes."

"What kind of books?"

"Marriage ones. Guides on how to win someone back, how to become irresistible to the opposite sex," Cooper said, rattling off some of their finds. "You'd be amazed at how much of that kind of stuff there is. We were searching on Amazon.com last night, and there were hundreds of titles!"

"Not to be overly negative, but you haven't exactly had very good luck with your own love life. Are you sure you're up to the task of helping others?" Alex asked Cooper.

"Do you have any other bright ideas?" she shot back.

"Not really." Alex shrugged.

"Then why don't you plan to make yourself useful and come with us to the bookstore after school," Cooper suggested. "We could really use a male perspective. And since you so kindly pointed out that I don't have a man in my life right now, you're the only one I can think of to drag along."

"I only said your love life wasn't that successful right now, I didn't say you don't have a guy. There's always Micah," Alex teased. "This could be a nice little predate outing for the two of you."

"Wow! You're so funny, you really should consider giving up your dream of film for a career in stand-up comedy instead," Cooper teased right back. When she saw the sad look on Claire's face, though, she became a little less jovial. "Actually, this whole thing has helped put my impending date with Micah in perspective. It's just one night out of my life, and I'm sure it will be fine. There are much worse ways to spend a Saturday night."

"It's a good thing you have such a great attitude about it, because Micah's right over there across the quad. And if I'm not mistaken, he's headed this way," Alex said as soon as Cooper had finished her little declaration.

"Alex, if you're joking I'm going to have to kill you in a very slow and painful way. You realize that, don't you?" Cooper said from between clenched teeth. She didn't want to look up and verify her friend's statement, because if it was true, then Micah would surely notice and think they were talking about him. Of course they were, but not in the way he would naturally assume. This would just convince him Cooper was more in love with him than ever. Oh, if only she'd had a reason to turn down his date in the first place! There were too many other things going on in her life right now without her having to deal with this.

"I don't think your committing murder will be necessary in this case," Alex fired back.

"Who's committing murder?" a newly familiar voice asked.

Cooper didn't even have to look up to see who it was. She shielded her eyes, though, and peered up at Micah, who stood towering over the group, smiling down at them as if he were doing them a favor by showering them with his charismatic presence.

"No one's committing murder," Cooper finally answered after a quick mental pep talk where she reminded herself that this, too, would pass. She consoled herself with the thought that someone as self-absorbed as Micah wouldn't be content to hang around people who didn't lavish him with praise for long.

"Well, that's good. I'd hate to have a little thing like a felony mess up our theater plans next week."

"If only it were that easy," Alex mumbled under his breath, mirroring Cooper's thoughts, too. Before she could suppress it, a little laugh erupted from somewhere deep inside her, and she and Alex shared a conspiratorial grin.

"What?" Micah asked, not understanding the joke.

To make matters worse, Claire was giving them one of her admonishing looks that meant she thought they were behaving badly.

"I'm sorry," Cooper told Micah. "It was just something we were talking about before. And I feel pretty safe in assuring you that I will not be in jail next weekend for any reason."

"Good. Well, I just wanted to get your phone number so I can call you over the weekend or one night next week to work out the details. It's hard to talk in biology with Mr. Robbins breathing down my neck every second."

"Oh, um . . . sure," Cooper replied, feeling completely *un*sure. She wasn't trying to be mean, but gearing up for the date itself was enough for her to handle! Now she was going to have to talk to Micah on the phone, too?

"Okay, well, what is it?" Micah prodded when Cooper wasn't more forthcoming with the digits.

"Oh . . . right. Sorry," she stammered. Then before she could get out anything more, Alex chimed in with her phone number.

"Do you want the number for her cell phone, too?" he

added helpfully. "That way you could reach her anytime, day or night."

Cooper's eyes were shooting daggers at Alex, but he pretended to be oblivious.

"I don't know. Do you think I need your cell phone number? Are you hard to reach at home?" Micah asked.

"No, I'm not. Really. And the cell phone is mostly for work and emergencies. I didn't even give Alex the number. He found it out and uses it to torment me at the worst possible times—like in the middle of class because he knows I'm horrible about remembering to turn it off. He's even called me when we've been at the movies together!" Cooper continued. "He'll pretend he's going for popcorn and instead he'll run out to the lobby and call me. I'll have to dig through my purse for my phone while everyone around me glares at me. It's his sick idea of fun."

Cooper wasn't sure why she had rattled on like that except that she was nervous and uncomfortable talking to Micah, especially in front of her friends. At least her rambling might have the unintentional benefit of proving to Micah that he really didn't want to spend time with her after all.

"I'll call you on your regular phone then, and if I can't track you down that way, there's always class. Mr. Robbins will just have to understand."

Cooper nodded in agreement while she made a mental note to be home as much as possible during the coming week. She wanted to make sure Micah would have no reason to have to work out the details of their date in front of Josh. She was pretty sure she had lost any chance of ever getting Josh to reconsider resurrecting their relationship, but still, she didn't have to help Micah drive the final nails in its coffin.

"I guess I'll talk to you later, then," Micah said, holding up the scrap of paper with her phone number on it as proof of what he was saying.

"Okay, bye," Cooper called after him. He was already walking away, but at her words he turned and winked at her. Six months ago that gesture would have melted her heart, but now it just gave her a sick feeling way down in the pit of her stomach. Worse yet, she knew it wasn't Micah's fault. He was being perfectly nice, but because of Josh, there was no way she could just enjoy his attentions and go with it.

"That went well, don't you think?" Alex asked as soon as Micah was out of earshot.

"Sometimes you can be such a jerk, I wonder why I even bother with you," Cooper told him, taking out some of her frustration over the situation with Micah and what was going on with Claire's parents on Alex.

"You know you don't mean that," Claire said quietly.

"Yeah," Alex added.

"And you could be a little bit more of a friend," Claire told him, wiping the smug look off his face.

"We could both be better friends," Cooper agreed, "by not worrying so much about ourselves and focusing on Claire for once."

"I can't argue with that," Alex replied. "Now, where were we in planning the new-and-improved parent trap?"

"So you'll help?" Claire asked.

"Of course. You know I'm always up for a little mischief. And while I'm not entirely convinced we can come up with something that will work, I can't think of a better excuse to expend a bit of brainpower."

"In other words, if your parents don't stay together, it won't be for our lack of trying," Cooper said.

Claire shrugged before saying, "I guess that's all I can ask for."

❊   ❊   ❊

That afternoon at a table at Barnes & Noble, with books spread out in every possible direction, the trio tried to ignore the disapproving looks from staffers and tried to get some work done. There weren't any books on keeping your parents together, so they were instead faced with trying to figure out what Mr. and Mrs. Hughes were each missing from their relationship and then find the corresponding fix and adapt it to their unique situation. Some of the books seemed genuinely aimed at helping people repair their relationships for the long haul, but others were full of tricks and gimmicks. Claire was drawn to the first type of book, while Cooper and Alex pored over the others.

"It would be nice if we had time to do this over a longer period of time, but we don't," Alex reminded Claire when she wrinkled up her nose at his choice of reading material. "Remember, you said yourself your dad is out looking for a place to move into right this very minute, so we can't afford to be subtle."

"Maybe," Claire half agreed.

That was all the encouragement Alex needed. "So how do you feel about a trip to the emergency room?" he asked.

"Nothing too serious, but if we could just get you to come down with a mild case of pneumonia or maybe even mono or something—"

"What?!" Claire and Cooper cried in unison, cutting him off before he could finish his thought. He wasn't easily deterred, though.

"It says in this book that, and I quote, 'Getting your husband or wife in the same room with you is half the battle. Time together allows you both to remember what brought you close in the first place. Time spent with your estranged spouse in a crisis situation is even better. A sick child, while not something you would wish for, can renew a bond that both parties thought was broken for good.' "

"That's disgusting!" Claire said. "Who would listen to advice like that?"

"People who want to save their marriages?" Alex suggested.

"You mean desperate people with no common sense left," Cooper countered. She didn't mind being a little sneaky, but emergency rooms were out of the question.

"Okay, maybe that was a little overboard, but you guys have to admit that getting them together in some way is going to be key to any plan."

"Sure, I'd just prefer it isn't over my deathbed," Claire said.

"Fair enough," Alex agreed. "You'll have them together for at least as long as it takes for your dad to find a place to move into, so maybe we need to focus on making the most of that."

"Yeah!" Cooper said, her enthusiasm suddenly returning.

"One of those scary books did have a few rational sugges-
tions, like jog your husband's or wife's memory with photos
of the two of you in happier times."

"And remind them of stories just the two of you shared,"
Alex added, finding the passage Cooper had marked in a
book titled *Winning Ways: 10 Tips for Re-igniting Any Relationship*.

"Now, these are things I could actually do," Claire said,
catching her friends' vision for this new and improved plan.

"All we need to do is come up with an excuse for you to
get your parents reminiscing," Cooper said. "Maybe you
could pretend to help your dad pack and get him to go
through the family albums with you that way."

"Wait! I've got it! You have Miss Simon for history, don't
you?" Alex asked.

"Yeah, I have her right after you," Claire answered.
"Why?"

"Well, our class was given the option to do a genealogy
project instead of taking the final exam. I'm assuming she
made the same offer to your class," Alex continued.

"Of course she did," Claire admitted. "But it seems like a
lot of extra work, and unlike you, I do fine on tests. I prefer
things where there are right and wrong answers."

Claire still wasn't getting it, but Cooper understood where
Alex was going with this whole genealogy thing. She
couldn't believe how perfect it was. "This is it!" she cried,
causing several bookstore patrons to look in her direction.
"This is the plan we've been searching for!"

"*What* is it?" Claire asked, still looking confused.

"The genealogy project. You can ask your parents to help

you, and they'll both have to sit down together and talk about family and their ancestors' marriages that lasted for decades and decades," Cooper said, her excited words tumbling out so quickly she could barely keep up with them.

"And it will even give you an excuse to pull out a bunch of old pictures," Alex pointed out, "since we get extra credit for visual aids."

Finally Claire was beginning to catch on. Cooper noticed her eyes light up for the first time in nearly twenty-four hours. She almost seemed like her old self again. Now, if only their plan would work, she could look like that all the time again.

Cooper glanced sideways and studied her best friend more closely. Even though she was smiling, her eyes were red-rimmed and bloodshot, and the area beneath them was dark and shadowy despite the best attempts of Claire's concealer. Cooper felt a new urgency as she realized they had no choice. This plan had to work. It just had to.

"**WHAT DO YOU MEAN** he's already found a place and he's moving out this weekend?" Alex practically shouted when the girls delivered the devastating news before the first bell rang at school the next morning.

"You don't have to announce to the entire Hudson High student body that her parents are splitting up," Cooper admonished.

"I'm sorry," Alex said, and Cooper could tell by the tone of his voice that he wasn't just apologizing for talking so loud but also for the pain this whole situation was causing Claire.

When the girls remained quiet, Alex broke the silence again by saying, "Well, at least we still have the plan, right? So we lost the battle. We can still win the war. We have not yet begun to fight!"

Cooper looked at Claire to determine which of them was the best one to deliver the second wave of bad news. When her friend merely sighed sadly in response, Cooper knew it was up to her to do the honors.

"While we appreciate your military analogies, General," Cooper said, addressing Alex, "it looks like Operation Family

Tree was shot down over enemy lines. There were no survivors."

"What are you talking about?"

At this point Claire joined the conversation, chiming in with all the pertinent details.

"I was all set last night to put the plan into action," she began. "I had the genealogy book we found yesterday at the bookstore, and my parents were actually together in the kitchen making dinner—which was completely weird, but that's a whole other story. Anyway, I start setting the table and I'm thinking maybe the plan won't even be necessary, they seem to be getting along so well. But then before I can even get a bite of food in my mouth, let alone bring up the project, they announce that my dad found an apartment and he'll be moving out on Saturday."

"It makes me want to throw up every time I hear you say it," Cooper said sympathetically.

"So it was your family's own little version of the Last Supper and they didn't even warn you?"

"I guess you could look at it that way," Claire shrugged.

"But you can still ask them for help on the project," Alex said, unwilling to give up. "Maybe you could invite your dad over next week and not tell your mom about it. Then as you look at family pictures together for your project, their eyes will meet over your head and they'll suddenly realize it was all a big mistake."

"And the music will swell?" Cooper suggested. "Why do I get the feeling you're shooting a scene, not helping reunite Claire's parents?"

"I can't help it if I think in movie terms," Alex said a bit defensively. "Anyway, I can do that and be helpful at the same time."

"Except that she already brought up the genealogy idea and they flat out refused to participate," Cooper explained.

"What do you mean? How can parents refuse to help their daughter with a homework project? That goes against the laws of nature or something, doesn't it?"

"That may be, but they refused just the same," Cooper said.

"Not only that, but they're shipping me off to my grandmother's for the weekend!" Claire complained. "They said she'd be just the person to help with this kind of assignment, and it will be nice for me to be out of the apartment while my dad's moving so it won't 'upset me.'"

"They actually said that?" an incredulous Alex asked. "Like him being gone when you get back Sunday night will be any less upsetting?"

"Exactly!" Cooper agreed.

"I made that same point, but they just wouldn't listen. So now not only are my parents splitting up, but I'm being shipped out of town to work on a project I don't even want to do! And I love my grandmother, but there is absolutely nothing to do at her museum of a house. She's very sweet, but she still thinks I'm five. The last time I was there she tried to get me to take an afternoon nap. I'm surprised she doesn't still serve me my milk in one of those cups with a lid and a built-in straw so I won't spill!"

"It will be a good chance to catch up on your sleep," Cooper suggested unhelpfully.

"I don't think I'm going to get much sleep this weekend

no matter where I am," Claire replied.

"Well, we can still give you a memorable send-off," Alex said. "I plan to put my valuable homeroom time to good use today coming up with the perfect lineup for movie night tonight. I was already thinking we could start with—"

Before Alex could share the beginning of his plan for the upcoming triple feature, though, Claire interrupted with yet more bad news.

"I can't come over for video night. My dad is taking me out for a sort of farewell dinner, although he won't really say that's what it is. So we're doing that and then I have to go home and pack because my mother told my grandmother that I'd be on the early train."

"Wow, they really *are* anxious to get you out of town, aren't they?" Alex asked.

"It sure seems that way," Claire agreed.

"So I thought we'd go ahead and cancel movie night just this once," Cooper suggested, bracing herself for Alex's response. She had expected him to be understanding of Claire, but movie night was nearly sacred. For her to miss just because she wasn't in the mood would surely invite a lecture on the importance of film and friendship.

That's why Cooper was completely stunned when Alex merely answered her with, "Sure. I'm not really in the mood to watch anything."

The girls looked at each other in alarm. They couldn't remember the last time Alex had not been in the mood for a movie. Since nothing else in their lives was normal, though, Cooper decided maybe Alex's response was fitting in light of the circumstances, and she breathed a huge sigh of relief over averting a fight on this subject, at least.

On the walk home from school that afternoon, the trio was a somber one. No one seemed to know what to say, so they all walked in silence, their steps resembling a funeral march. Only when Alex had to turn to head toward the subway station did the group finally speak.

"I'm not ready to give up just yet," Alex assured Claire. "I'm going to spend the entire weekend searching that book we bought for a better plan."

The book he was referring to was one of three they had bought at the bookstore. Cooper, Claire, and Alex had not only pooled their cash to purchase the genealogy book for Claire to use in their master plan but also bought two of the better relationship books. To keep Claire's parents from discovering what they were up to, Cooper and Alex each took one of the volumes home.

"I'll do the same with my book," Cooper agreed, thankful to have something to occupy the hours that were threatening to stretch before her during the weekend without her friend.

"Maybe you guys can get together at Cuppa Joe tomorrow and compare notes," Claire suggested. It was just like her to think of them even with all that was on her mind.

"Sure, we could do that," Cooper and Alex both said at the same time.

"I guess I'll see you on Monday," Alex added, seeming suddenly hesitant to leave but uncomfortable just standing there. After shifting back and forth from foot to foot several times, he quickly gave Claire a hug and then turned to leave. He was already several feet away when he turned back to shout, "Call me if you need anything—no matter what time it is! I'll be praying for you!"

Now that the silence had been broken, Cooper found she had several things she wanted to say herself.

"I hope you know you can call me, too. Or if you need to come over after dinner tonight just to talk, I'll be around. I could even take the train to your grandmother's with you, just so you aren't alone on the way there. I'm sure there's another train returning to Manhattan right after and I could take it right back. Your grandma and your parents wouldn't even have to know."

"Thanks, but you don't have to do that. I'm sure I'll be fine. I will call you after dinner tonight, though, and let you know how it went. And I'll take my laptop with me so we can always email or send each other instant messages if we really need to communicate. That way if we're typing instead of talking, my grandmother can't hear anything we might say about getting my parents back together and about your plan."

"That makes sense," Cooper agreed. "I'll be sure to check my email regularly."

When Claire got ready to exit the elevator on her floor, Cooper felt like she should give her a big hug, too. It seemed like they were saying good-bye forever, but Cooper couldn't figure out why. They'd spent weekends apart before. Usually under happier circumstances, but still. It wasn't until she was in her own apartment that Cooper realized that in their own way, both she and Alex were being forced to say good-bye to the Hugheses' marriage and let go of it, as well. Their breakup wasn't just affecting their own family, it was like those ripples in a pond when you throw a stone in. Of course, Claire and her parents were the ones whose lives were being rocked the most by these newly created waves, but the concentric rings fanned out to affect others like Cooper, shaking their formerly calm world. Cooper wanted so badly to do anything she could to make the water's surface smooth again, but she didn't know how. Still, she found herself face down on her bed asking God how to go back in time and stop that first rock from being thrown in.

Her heart-wrenching prayers were interrupted by the ringing of her cell phone. Cooper frantically fished in her backpack for the tiny gadget, sure that whoever was on the other end of the line would give up before she could answer. Finally her fingers felt the familiar shape and she hit "talk" before she could even see the button.

"Hello?" she breathlessly spoke into the phone.

"Cooper?" the voice on the other end of the line asked. Before she even identified herself, Cooper knew who it was and she immediately began apologizing.

"Tara! I'm so sorry I forgot to check in. It's been a horrible few days. My best friend's parents are—"

Cooper wasn't allowed to finish, though, before Tara was interrupting with the address of a go-see Cooper needed to be at in ten minutes.

"Did you write that down?" Tara asked when she was done giving directions.

"Yes, I've got it. I'll leave right now. If I can catch a cab right away I may only be a minute or two late."

"That's my girl. Now hurry!" the agent instructed. "Oh,

UNMISTAKABLY COOPER ELLIS

but don't forget to relax. When you're too nervous you don't smile. Don't forget to smile."

"I won't," Cooper promised before hanging up the phone. She then quickly pulled the T-shirt she had worn that day over her head and threw on a black-and-gray–striped turtleneck instead. Then she grabbed her backpack and her "book" that contained photos of her from previous modeling jobs and raced out the door. She was locking the dead bolt when she realized she forgot to leave her parents a note telling them where she was. Oh well. It was too late now. She could call once she got to the appointment and leave a message on the machine at home.

Fortunately, Cooper snagged a cab as soon as she walked out the door of her apartment building. If it had been thirty minutes later, there wouldn't be a cab to be found, since the usually crowded New York City streets became impossible to maneuver during rush hour on Fridays. As the cab sped along the busy streets, she pulled out her small makeup bag and applied a little plummy lipstick and some pale pressed powder on her nose and chin, then brushed her hair with quick, hard strokes. After that she barely had time to pop an Altoid before she had reached her destination. She gathered up her things, stuffed a five-dollar bill through the plastic partition to the driver, and raced up to the eighteenth-floor lobby.

Only after she had checked in with the receptionist and been told to have a seat did she finally start breathing again. Before she got too relaxed, though, she remembered she still had to call home and check in, and then there was nothing to do but wait. Cooper killed time scanning the room, looking at the other girls assembled and trying to guess from the types that had been called in what the shoot was for. It could be anything from a fashion layout in a teen magazine (Cooper had been told on several occasions that her look wasn't "mature" enough to get her jobs at the bigger fashion magazines, she was more of a girl next door) to an ad for zit cream or makeup. It didn't really matter since Cooper wasn't too picky. The only work she really didn't want to do was an ad for any kind of feminine hygiene product. It was one thing to have your face connected with broken-out skin, but she knew if she ever did a minipad ad that the teasing at school would be endless. She'd have to persuade her parents to homeschool her. Her social life would be over.

Fortunately, the job was an ad for a new clothing line. Cooper wasn't sure how she did, but she remembered what Tara had said and made sure to smile. She couldn't do much more than that. If she'd learned anything since she'd started modeling, it was that it was a very subjective business. She couldn't make her eyes less gray or her teeth smaller or her legs longer, and if that's what someone wanted, she'd just have to accept that she wasn't going to get that job.

She called Tara once she got home just to let her know she had made it in time and was surprised to find out that her booker had already received word that Cooper had indeed been hired. She would need to be there Monday right after school. Cooper made a note in her appointment book and promised she wouldn't forget. At least *something* in her life was going right.

COOPER'S PARENTS CALLED shortly after she returned home to say they were going to meet for an early dinner and a movie and would be home before ten. It felt weird that her parents were continuing on with their Friday night dinner-and-a-movie ritual as if nothing had happened. Her parents and Claire's had always gone out together on Friday nights before, and it was strange now that they were breaking up to have things seem so different yet the same all at once.

Cooper knew it wouldn't do her any good to dwell on all the yucky stuff that was going on, though. She figured she might as well try to do something useful so she popped some microwave popcorn, grabbed a can of Coke from the fridge, and retrieved the copy of *Marriage CPR* from its hiding place under the bed. The book had a cheesy cover with a wedding picture on a gurney being shocked with those paddles they were always using on *ER* to restart people's hearts. But once you got past that, the advice was pretty good—compared to what was in the other books they had looked at.

An hour later Cooper was still on the couch, nestled cozily under a fuzzy blanket, the popcorn long since eaten, and her empty Coke can discarded on the coffee table. She was reading one of the many case studies in the book, and the couple seemed so similar to the Hugheses that she was completely caught up. In fact, she was so engrossed in what she was reading that she didn't hear the key in the lock until it was too late. She only had time to look up before she saw her father enter the apartment.

"Hi, honey," her dad said as if he wasn't supposed to be at dinner or a movie.

"What are you doing home?" Cooper asked, slipping the book between the couch cushions as she did so. The trick wouldn't have worked with her mother, who noticed everything, but her dad wasn't nearly so observant. Still, Cooper found herself holding her breath as he approached.

"Your mom and I got all the way to the restaurant and had even ordered an appetizer when we both admitted it just didn't feel right to be out. Neither one of us was in the mood to have fun, so we decided to cut the evening short. Your mom stopped downstairs at the Hugheses', but she should be up in a little bit," her dad explained.

"Yeah, I wasn't in the mood to do anything, either," Cooper admitted.

"Well, whatever you were reading when I came in seemed to be holding your attention pretty well. What was it?" Mr. Ellis asked as he fished out the book from its hiding place.

"Oh, um . . . it's nothing," Cooper stammered, scrambling for an explanation that would sound plausible, wouldn't be a lie, and most important of all, wouldn't give away their plan.

"Marriage CPR?" her dad asked, his eyebrow raised questioningly.

Since Cooper hadn't come up with anything yet that fit all three of her explanation criteria, she merely shrugged and hoped her dad would let it go. Unfortunately, she had no such luck.

"Where did you get this?" her dad persisted.

"At the bookstore," Cooper admitted.

"You bought a book called *Marriage CPR?*" he asked again, still not understanding why.

"Well, you're always encouraging me to read more and to expand my horizons. I've never read anything on this subject, and it's really very interesting," Cooper said, trying her best to look innocent. "You'd be surprised."

"I'm sure I would be, but I bet the surprise has less to do with what's in the book and more to do with what's behind it. Now, what exactly are you doing with a marriage book?" her dad asked again.

"Oh, all right, but you know, you sound like you've been taking lessons from Mom, and I don't mean that as a compliment," Cooper said a little too defiantly.

"Watch it, young lady," her dad warned.

She always knew she was in trouble when he called her that, so she finally came clean. She told him about their plan and the books and the genealogy project. When every last detail had been divulged, Cooper shook her head sadly and said, "I'd make a horrible POW. At the first sign of torture, I'd completely cave. I even found myself almost starting to confess to you about that time in third grade when I used your toothbrush on the cat." The words were barely out of her mouth when Cooper covered the offending facial feature with her hand. A muffled "oops" soon followed.

"You did *what?*" her dad asked, momentarily distracted from the bigger issue at hand.

"It was a long time ago," Cooper reminded him, knowing it was a lame defense.

"You're just lucky I didn't come down with some horrible feline disease," her dad admonished before letting her off the hook just a little.

"Well, you have to give me credit for taking Mr. Whiskers' oral hygiene so seriously," Cooper added, causing her dad to warn her not to push her luck. "If that's all, I think I'm going to go to my room," Cooper said, rising from the couch and stretching in an exaggerated way. She almost threw in a yawn for effect but decided at the last minute that might be overdoing it. It didn't matter. It was barely dark out, something that didn't escape her dad's notice, and he was nowhere near done discussing *Marriage CPR.*

"I know this whole thing must be very difficult for you," Mr. Ellis began, and Cooper knew then that she might as well sit back down. With a sigh she plopped down on the couch and pulled one of her knees up to her chest. "That doesn't give you license to meddle in other people's lives. I understand that Claire is your friend, but that still doesn't give you the right. This whole thing is hard enough on everyone as it is."

"So what are we supposed to do, just sit back and let Claire's dad leave?" Cooper asked, feeling the tears that had threatened all day beginning to gather again in the corners of her eyes.

"If that's the decision he's made, then yes."

"So you're not even going to try to talk him out of it?" Cooper cried. "He's your best friend. Can't you tell him he's making a huge mistake?"

It wasn't until just then that Cooper realized how tired her father looked. His eyes were bloodshot, and the usually faint wrinkles on his forehead were more pronounced, as if he had been furrowing his brow all day long. When he spoke again, his voice sounded tired, too.

"Honey, don't you think I've tried? This didn't happen overnight, even though I know it seems that way to you. I've talked until I was blue in the face. Your mom has, too. I wish it were as simple as reading a book or showing them a few pictures from happier times, but it isn't. I'm sorry."

"I'm sorry, too," Cooper sniffed, then wiped her nose on her sleeve, not caring if it was considered rude.

Then just when Cooper was sure things couldn't get any worse, they did. "I hope you know that just because this happened to Claire's parents doesn't mean it's going to happen to your mother and me," her father continued.

Cooper was sure she felt her heart stop beating in her chest. At the exact same time, the blood in her veins turned to ice water. She hadn't even considered her own parents splitting up! Even though most of the kids at school had divorced parents and all sorts of different stepmoms or dads—not to mention step or half siblings—she had never really considered that it could happen to her. Of course, neither had Claire until that week. Now she had a whole new worry. Why would her father have even brought it up if it wasn't a possibility?

"Cooper?" her dad asked.

"Yeah?" she glumly replied.

"You believe me, don't you?"

"I don't know," Cooper answered honestly. "If it could happen to Claire's parents, it could happen to anyone."

"You're right, and it's important to realize that. It's when you think something can never happen to you that you're in the most danger of that very thing happening because you're not on your guard."

Cooper was still trying to wrap her mind around what he was saying when he continued. "Now, you know your mother and I have our problems, but we are both committed to always working them through. We know all too well how easy it is to let things go, so we fight very hard not to let that happen in our relationship," her dad explained.

"Why didn't Mr. and Mrs. Hughes fight against that, too?" Cooper wondered aloud.

"I don't know, sweetie. I wish I had an answer for you."

"I wish you did, too. It would sure make things a lot easier."

After an extra-long hug from her dad, Cooper gathered up her things and headed for her bedroom. There didn't seem to be any reason to keep reading the marriage book now since her parents had revoked her matchmaker license. She decided to trade it in for something a little lighter.

When her mother poked her head into Cooper's room a while later, Cooper was under the covers reading the good parts from *Emma*. She loved not just the ending but also the exchanges between Emma and Mr. Knightley. Rereading those well-crafted words helped restore a little of her faith in lasting love, which was something she really needed that night.

"Your dad told me about your little talk tonight," Mrs. Ellis announced from the doorway.

"Oh," Cooper squirmed, feeling uncomfortable all over again.

"Let me just reiterate what your father told you: I do not want you interfering in any way with the Hugheses' marriage. Be concerned about Claire, but leave them alone."

"I know," Cooper sighed. "Dad already told me."

"Good. I just hope you got the message loud and clear."

"I did."

Before her mother could say any more, the phone rang.

"Saved by the bell," Cooper said, smiling at her mother before adding, "I'll get it since I'm sure it's for me."

Cooper scrambled for the phone, but she waited until her mother was out of the room before hitting the "talk" button. She didn't want her parents overhearing her conversation with Claire even though she no longer had any secrets.

"Okay, so how did it go? Tell me everything," Cooper began before even greeting her friend.

"I'd be happy to tell you everything if I knew what we were talking about," an unfamiliar male voice said. It wasn't Alex or Mr. Hughes, and Cooper couldn't think of anyone else who would be calling, especially so late.

"Excuse me, but who am I speaking with?" Cooper asked, suddenly turning formal.

"This is Micah. Who am *I* speaking with?"

Micah?! Cooper felt her cheeks burning bright pink and rolled her eyes at her mistake. Why did these things always happen to her? She was always getting herself into messes like this. She would need to learn to be a little more cautious if she were to avoid these embarrassing situations in the future. That didn't help her right now, though.

"Oh, hi, Micah. This is Cooper. I thought you were someone else," Cooper sheepishly explained.

"Obviously. Do you always try to guess who's on the phone before you answer it?"

"No," Cooper replied, wishing he'd just drop the whole thing but knowing that wasn't likely to happen. Instead, she took a deep breath and began explaining.

"I'm sorry I'm not Claire," Micah said when Cooper had finished her story. "Next time I'll say my name right away before you can even get a word in so you won't say anything you don't mean to."

"Gee, thanks."

"No problem. Now, about next weekend, I was wondering what kind of food you like. There's a little French bistro my mom swears is great, or there's always Italian. What do you think? I thought I'd better go ahead and make a reservation now since anything in the theater district is going to be packed just before show time."

"French and Italian both sound fine," Cooper answered noncommittally.

"Okay, I'll try the French first and if we can't get in there, then we'll go Italian."

"That works for me."

After that, there was an awkward pause until Micah thought to ask for Cooper's address. "Since curtain is at 8:00, we probably need to get to the restaurant around 6:00, so I thought I'd pick you up about 5:45. I just need to know where you live."

"Oh sure," Cooper agreed. Before she could give him the address, though, her call waiting beeped in. Not wanting to keep Claire waiting, Cooper asked Micah if she could just give him the address at school the next week and thankfully he agreed. As soon as he did, Cooper pushed the button that banished Micah and brought her into contact with Claire. Before she embarrassed herself again, though, she made sure the person on the other end of the line identified herself.

"Claire, is that you?"

"Of course it's me. Who else would it be?"

"The way tonight's been going, it could be just about anybody," Cooper said before explaining in greater detail.

"So Micah called you already?" Claire asked.

"Yes, but I hung up on him to talk to you."

"That's hardly a supreme sacrifice since you didn't want to talk to him in the first place."

"But it's the thought that counts, right?" Cooper said. "Besides, I wanted to hear how your dinner went. Was it as awful as you thought it was going to be?"

"Not quite," Claire said. "We actually had a really nice talk. And then he brought up the subject of visitation."

"What do you mean by 'visitation'?" Cooper asked, not liking the sound of that one bit.

"It means that my dad wants me to come stay with him one night a week and every other weekend," Claire explained.

"No!" Cooper's mouth cried before her brain could stop it.

"I know. That was my reaction, too, but he's my dad. I can't just not see him. So I told him I'd give it a try, but that I can change my mind at any time."

"So will you have your own room at his apartment?"

"Sort of. The place is furnished, and the spare room is a sort of study/guest room. He says it's really nice and there's plenty of room for me to stay. He also said I could decorate it however I wanted."

"Was that weird talking about decorating an apartment that your mom won't be living in?"

"Definitely. I just kept trying not to let myself think of things like that."

"I'm sorry for bringing it up, then," Cooper apologized. "I was just curious."

"I know. So am I. It's fine. Or it will be. Things are so tense around here, I'll almost be glad when it's over," Claire confided in a voice barely above a whisper. "And another thing: I'd never admit it to my parents, but I'm glad I won't have to be here to watch my dad move out. Tonight was emotional enough. I can't wait to get away."

"I wish there was something I could do to make it easier on you," Cooper said, meaning the words so much it made her heart hurt.

"You are doing something. You're being a friend and you're listening. That means a lot."

"It doesn't seem like enough," Cooper admitted.

"For now, it will have to be."

MONDAY AFTER SCHOOL Cooper raced to the subway, not wanting to be late to her modeling job. As she stood on the underground platform waiting for the train, she breathed a sigh of relief at how normal the day had been. Claire had returned the night before with the genealogy report under one arm and a Tupperware container of oatmeal cookies under the other. Her grandmother had spoiled her rotten all weekend. And while she told Cooper and Alex that it hadn't softened the blow of her parents' impending divorce, it had allowed her to escape that painful reality for a while. And now that the first night in the apartment without her dad was over, she felt sure she'd survive. They'd all survive. Things wouldn't ever be the same, but they'd find some new range of normal.

The train *clickety-clacking* noisily into the station brought Cooper back to the present. She hopped on board and took a seat, then busied herself making up life stories to go with each of the other passengers in her car. It kept her occupied until she arrived at her stop, which she was alerted to by the street number etched into the old Art Deco tile once they pulled into the station, not by the muffled, incoherent announcement of the driver. Cooper wondered why they even bothered to use the intercom system. It always sounded like they were talking underwater in a tunnel while wearing a scuba mask.

For once, Cooper easily found the address Tara had given her the previous week, and when she entered the featureless room she was pleasantly surprised to see a somewhat familiar face.

"Lindsay, right?" Cooper asked.

"Bible-reading girl!" Linsday replied, hugging Cooper as if they were long-lost friends.

"Uh . . . yeah, I guess that's me," Cooper said, feeling a little uncomfortable at the admission and then feeling guilty for her unease with the spiritual moniker.

"What's your real name again?"

"It's Cooper. Ellis."

"Oh yeah. I remember now. You're not any relation to Perry Ellis, the designer, are you?" Lindsay asked, then before Cooper could answer, she added, "I didn't already ask you that, did I?"

"No, I don't think so, and no, I don't think so," Cooper replied.

Then for the next few minutes Lindsay continued to chatter away as if she'd just downed a double espresso. Cooper wondered where her new friend got her energy. After a long day at school, all Cooper wanted to do was take a nap or plop down in front of the TV. Lindsay didn't stop talking until the stylist approached and introduced herself.

"Hi, I'm Lauren, and if we're going to get the shots we

need while there's still any kind of light left, we'd better get going."

"Lindsay, Jonathan is ready to do your makeup, and, Cooper, why don't you go see what Stefan has in mind for your hair today?"

It wasn't until they were in the makeshift dressing room more than an hour later that Cooper saw Lindsay again. There were also two other girls crowded into an area that was no bigger than Cooper's closet at home. All those bodies made it difficult to see what they were putting on, but Cooper paused when she came to a sheer pink concoction she could only assume was supposed to be a blouse. Not that it looked like a blouse or anything, but the sleeves were a giveaway. Cooper had seen some pretty strange stuff masquerading as fashion since she'd started working for Yakomina Models, but this bordered on being obscene. There was no way she could wear it in front of the few people in the room, let alone in a picture that would appear in national magazines!

"Hey, are you coming?" Lindsay asked from the opening in the curtain that led back out into the main room.

"Tell them I'll be there in just a minute," Cooper replied.

Before Lindsay had even walked away, Cooper was fishing her cell phone out of her bag. She dialed Tara first, but she wasn't in the office. She tried Tara's cell phone, but she just got an annoying message that said, "This cellular customer is out of range." Next Cooper called her mom, but with the same results. Then she remembered her mother saying something that morning about a day trip to Connecticut for work. She and Claire's mom were going together "to help get her mind off things," Mrs. Ellis had said. That still didn't

117

explain why her cell phone wasn't working, unless they were really far out in the country. It didn't matter, though. Wherever she was, the end result was the same: Cooper had to handle the situation all by herself.

Slowly she emerged from the dressing room, wearing the skirt they had given her and her own shirt. She was holding the offending pink garment as if it were a disease she was afraid she might somehow catch.

"Cooper, why aren't you dressed?" Lauren asked, her voice laced with impatience. "Is there some sort of problem?"

"Actually, there is," Cooper said while simultaneously praying that God would give her the strength to stand up for her beliefs. It was hard with a roomful of adults looking at you disapprovingly, and for a moment Cooper felt herself begin to waver. But then she tried to imagine everyone at school, not to mention people at church, seeing pictures of her in that revealing blouse and her convictions were renewed.

"I can't wear this unless you have some sort of tank top to go under it or something. You can see my bra—and everything else!—right through the fabric," Cooper explained, willing her voice to remain calm.

"With the lighting we're using, it won't appear that sheer in the photos," Lauren assured her, patting her arm condescendingly as she did so. "Now, why don't you go slip it on and we'll get started."

Cooper wasn't convinced. "How can light shining on it make it less sheer?" she persisted.

"Oh, I didn't know we had an amateur photographer in

our midst," the stylist all but sneered. "When did you become an expert on lighting?"

"I . . . I . . . I'm not," Cooper stammered. "I just don't feel comfortable wearing such a revealing blouse. I'm not trying to be difficult. Really."

"Well, I'm just trying to get my job done," Lauren shot back. "I can't believe you managed to get other work with this sort of unprofessional attitude. If you're going to be this picky, you're never going to make it in this business."

"But I'm *not* being picky," Cooper insisted, knowing her assertion was falling on deaf ears.

"It sure seems that way to me, and in the meantime you're wasting valuable shooting time."

"If it were just a matter of what I liked or didn't like, this wouldn't even be an issue, but that's not it," Cooper continued. "I just can't wear that blouse. I'm really sorry, but I can't."

When she finished her little speech, Cooper felt sick to her stomach. She knew that Lauren was probably going to fire her on the spot, and she couldn't really blame her. The stylist needed to get her job done, after all. But it seemed so supremely unfair. *Why does doing the right thing always have to be so hard?* Cooper wondered.

Just as Lauren opened her mouth to speak and Cooper braced herself for the words she knew were coming, Lindsay unexpectedly stepped forward. "I'll wear that blouse," she volunteered. "The one I'm wearing will look better with Cooper's eyes anyway."

Before Lauren could even agree, Lindsay was walking to the dressing room, undoing her buttons as she went. Cooper looked uncertainly at Lauren before following the other model and making the trade.

"I owe you sooooo big," Cooper told Lindsay once they were alone behind the curtain.

"Don't worry about it. It wasn't a big deal," Lindsay said, dismissing the good deed with a wave of her hand.

"No, really, you saved my life out there," Cooper continued. "You don't know how much this means to me." She was even more touched by the other girl's actions because so many of the models she had met were really catty and would never risk losing favor with an employer to help out another girl. They took the job very seriously, and they weren't about to let anyone get in their way, especially an unknown like Cooper.

"Well, since you put it that way, maybe I'll let you do something for me one day," Lindsay said before the two girls emerged, the clothing swap complete.

"Anything," Cooper whispered as they walked across the room to face the music with Lauren. "You just name it."

The rest of the shoot was uncomfortable, but it passed without any other major problems. Still, Cooper knew she had definitely burned a professional bridge. Not only was she stuck in the back of almost every shot, but many of the poses the photographer suggested—with Lauren's guidance—had Cooper practically obscured from view.

As if that wasn't bad enough, Lauren made it abundantly clear that she would never hire Cooper again and she wouldn't stop there. She would encourage her friends and colleagues to do the same.

The second the shoot was over, Cooper changed back

into her own clothes faster than someone dressing to escape a burning building. She found she couldn't get out of that room fast enough. When she reached the door, though, she paused and pulled out a scrap of paper from her backpack. After locating a pen, she scrawled her name and phone number, then went over to where Lindsay was sitting on the floor, zipping up her knee-length black boots.

"Here. I wanted to give you this," Cooper said, holding out the piece of paper to Lindsay. "And I meant what I said. I owe you, so if you ever need anything, anything at all, just call me."

Linsday took the scrap and tucked it in the pocket of her designer pants. Cooper doubted there was anything she had that this girl needed, but her offer was genuine and she was glad she'd made it. She was even more glad when she was out on the street breathing in the polluted New York City air in big gulps. What a day!

THE REST OF THE WEEK seemed to drag on. It was as if the hands of every clock in the city were weighed down so they could move only half as fast as they were meant to. It wouldn't have been as bad if Cooper weren't so anxious to get her date with Micah over with. He had been making a point to hang around her desk whenever he could during biology. While the attention was flattering, she couldn't enjoy it because she was too busy calculating the damage each little in-class encounter was doing to her already tenuous relationship with Josh.

Cooper wanted so badly to just pull Josh aside and tell him that there was nothing between her and Micah, but what reason did he have to believe her? She wouldn't believe her if she were in Josh's place. He already knew she used to have a big crush on Micah, he'd heard her agree to go on a date with him, and now they were talking to each other every day in class. What was Josh supposed to think?

The situation only got worse as the day of the big date got closer. On Friday, Micah approached Cooper while she and Josh were busy with a lab assignment, causing her to inwardly groan. Things had been going well between her and Josh, and she was busily looking for an opening to bring up Micah and at least drop a hint that she wasn't interested anymore. Even if Josh didn't believe her, at least she would know she had said it. That would make *her* feel better.

Feeling better just wasn't meant to be, though. As Micah came near, he slung an arm possessively over her shoulder and leaned in close before announcing that he needed her address so he could pick her up the next night. She tried to politely put some distance between them, but there was no nice way to do it. All she could do was squirm a little and hope he got the hint—or at least that Josh would look at her face and see that the relationship was one-sided.

"That's not too far from here," Micah pointed out after Cooper had explained where she lived. She wasn't sure whose benefit he was saying that for since she obviously knew the distance to her apartment.

"Well, I guess I'll see you tomorrow night," Micah said before turning to go. Cooper was just about to let out the breath she'd been holding, waiting for things to go from bad to worse, when Micah turned back toward her. "Oh, and I decided to go with Italian food. I hope that's okay."

Cooper nodded agreeably, hoping that would hurry Micah along. Instead, it just seemed to encourage him to stay.

"Since the theater's near The Village, I made a reservation at this place my brother recommended. It's called The Grand something or other. I don't remember exactly, but it's near Washington Square Park."

Cooper felt her heart sink down into her toes. Surely this couldn't be happening. *Please, God, tell me this isn't happening*, she pleaded. But the look on Josh's face told her it was.

"You don't mean the Grand Ticino, do you?" Cooper asked, although somewhere in her gut she already knew the answer.

"Yeah! That's the place," Micah proudly replied. "You've heard of it before? It must be more popular than I thought."

Heard of it? The Grand Ticino was where Josh had taken Cooper on their first date—her first real date with anyone ever. She couldn't believe that the memory would now be tainted by Micah and the date she didn't even want. It was all she could do not to run screaming from the room.

Somehow Cooper managed to maintain control long enough to say, "Excuse me, but I think I need to go to the rest room." Before Micah or Josh could respond, she hurried up to Mr. Robbins' desk and grabbed the pass before rushing to the stairs. She took them two at a time, determined to make it to the girls' bathroom before the tears began to flow.

❄   ❄   ❄

"He's taking you where?" Claire said at lunch, displaying the same amount of shock and horror Cooper had felt just thirty minutes earlier. "That's awful!"

"Thanks," Cooper replied. It was amazing how much it helped just to have her friend's sympathy.

"That's stranger than even your life usually is," Alex added, incredulous.

"Thanks for noticing," Cooper shot back before turning to Claire again and pleadingly asking, "Now, are you still sure there's no way I can get out of this honestly? Maybe I could catch the mumps or find someone at school with the flu and ask them to breathe on me. It's worth a try, isn't it?

I'm desperate!" By now Cooper had a grip on Claire's shirt with both hands and was shaking her friend for effect.

"Even if you found someone contagious, I don't think most communicable diseases have an incubation period of thirty hours or less," Claire smiled.

"You *would* have to go and get practical on me at a time like this," Cooper complained, loosening her grip on the fabric of her friend's shirt.

"Someone's got to do it," Claire replied, sighing dramatically as if the burden of the world were on her shoulders.

"At least we can help you forget about Micah tonight," Alex offered.

"Yeah, movie night will cheer you up," Claire added.

"I don't know if anything can make me feel better," Cooper argued. "But I guess it can't make me feel any worse."

"Now, that's the sunny, positive Cooper Ellis we all know and love," Alex teased.

❋   ❋   ❋

Her friends were right. Movie night did help. Losing herself in someone else's life for several hours made her own problems seem, if not smaller, at least further away. And when Claire and Alex offered to come over the next day to offer fashion advice and moral support before her date, Cooper knew that with such good friends, she really had very little to complain about.

By Saturday night she wasn't feeling quite so certain. With Claire's help, she had chosen a gray beaded skirt and sweater with a matching camisole underneath. And since it was fairly warm out, she wore a pair of chunky sandals with bare legs.

"I want to tell you that you look great, but I don't know if that will make you feel better or worse," Claire fretted.

"It's fine," Cooper said. "And thanks."

"No problem. I just wish I could hang out with you until Micah gets here, but since this is my first weekend at my dad's new place, I feel like I should get back."

"We understand," Alex consoled. "And if it makes you feel any better, things will get less weird after a while. I promise."

"I'm not sure I want them to get less weird," Claire admitted. "I don't ever want my dad having his own place to feel normal to me."

"Well, maybe you won't have to get used to it. There's still the possibility that they'll get back together. You said yourself that they aren't planning to make any permanent decisions for a while."

"I know."

"In the meantime, you should go. And don't worry about me. I'll be fine. Besides, I have Alex here to keep me company until it's time to go," Cooper encouraged.

"I'd feel better if you didn't look like someone who was about to be led to the electric chair," Claire said, which prompted Cooper to plaster on her most fake beauty pageant contestant smile.

"Ugh!" Claire groaned. "That's hideous. Go ahead and look depressed after all. At least that way you won't frighten the other theatergoers."

"I thought that's what you'd say."

Claire was barely out the door when Cooper's mom appeared. As she took in the scene before her, she seemed alarmed.

"Alex isn't going to be here when your date arrives, is he?" she asked in a way that let Cooper know there was only one possible sensible answer.

Cooper was still busy trying to formulate her answer when Alex did it for her.

"Sure," he said. "I'm heading downtown anyway, so I thought I'd just tag along," he joked.

Mrs. Ellis wasn't amused.

"You're never going to get this boy to ask you out on another date that way," she said, unaware that that was exactly what her daughter wanted.

Of course Alex wouldn't be tagging along. He had done that once before without being invited. It had, not surprisingly, caused problems not just with their dates, but with their friendship, as well. It was nice that they could joke about it now, even if that joke was sort of at her mother's expense.

"Oh well, I suppose it is your life. At some point you're going to have to make your own decisions," her mother finally said, the signal that she was giving up—at least for now.

Unfortunately, Cooper was learning that along with the freedom to do what she wanted came the responsibility for opening the door when the doorbell rang a few minutes later. She checked her teeth in the entryway mirror to make sure none of her lipstick had slid onto them. Then, after taking a deep, cleansing breath, she opened the door and greeted her date.

While there was a smile on her face that even her mother couldn't have found fault with, in the back of her mind all she could think about was how being an adult was way overrated.

COOPER COULDN'T REALLY FIND fault with much about the evening. Micah was easier to be around when he was away from school and his friends. And while she noticed the food at the Grand Ticino didn't taste quite as good as when she'd been in Josh's company, she couldn't really blame that on Micah. Even the play was mildly interesting. The theater was little and cramped, but it meant the audience was closer to the actors, which worked well for the conversational sort of show they were doing about a group of musicians living in Greenwich Village in the 1950s.

Even though the evening hadn't been a complete disaster, as Cooper walked with Micah up Fifth Avenue, she was calculating how many minutes until she'd be home in her own bed. Not that she wanted to hurt Micah's feelings, they just didn't have anything in common, which she hoped was something he now saw, as well. Surely he'd noticed the awkward pauses and how she'd had nothing to add to his conversation about international soccer and the World Cup or choosing a college—something she didn't have to do for almost two years. In return, he'd stared blankly at her stories of weekends spent with Claire and Alex watching movies or hanging out in the park.

On the subway ride back to her apartment, Micah tried one last time to connect.

"So are you a Mets or a Yankees fan?" he asked, looking at Cooper as if this one answer would hold the key to her personality.

"I don't really know," Cooper shrugged. "I've been to a few Yankees games with my dad, but I don't really follow baseball much. If I had to pick a team, I guess it would be the Dodgers. I saw a game in L.A. once and really liked the stadium."

"The Dodgers?! But they left New York and deserted their fans! You can't like the Dodgers!" Micah complained, seeming to take her answer as a personal insult.

"Sorry?" Cooper ventured, not sure exactly what she was apologizing for, but doing it, all the same.

"It's just that it doesn't make any sense," he continued. "You'd be better off not liking any team than liking the Dodgers."

"You're the one who asked," Cooper reminded him. As she did so, she noticed Micah looked sorry that he'd ever brought it up.

The pair rode in silence the rest of the way, not talking again until they were staring at the door to the Ellises' apartment.

"Well, thanks," Cooper said, her hand on the doorknob, ready to make her escape.

"You're very welcome," Micah replied.

Then before Cooper had a chance to move away, Micah's

face was next to hers and his lips were continuing to come closer. There was no time to get out of the way, but at the last minute she was able to move her face so that his kiss landed just below her eye. It was, like the entire evening, awkward—but Cooper wasn't about to feel obligated to kiss someone back just because he'd bought her dinner.

"Well, good night," Cooper said, leaving a stunned Micah on her doorstep.

"Good night," he managed to murmur just before she closed the door.

Cooper went to bed that night feeling satisfied that she had kept her word—and that she could be reasonably certain Micah would be showering his attention on some other "lucky" girl by the time they returned to school on Monday.

❊   ❊   ❊

The morning after her big date, Cooper was trying to decide if she wanted to change out of the black dress she had worn to church into something a bit more casual before meeting Claire and Alex at Cuppa Joe, when the ringing of the phone interrupted her fashion dilemma. She was sure it was one or the other of her friends, letting her know they were ready and waiting on her. She had learned her lesson after her conversation with Micah, though, and carefully said, "Hello?"

"Cooper, it's Josh."

She felt her heart jump up into her throat, blocking her airway and making it impossible for her to speak. Why was Josh calling her now, after all this time?

"Cooper? Are you there?"

Cooper swallowed hard several times in succession, which finally made it possible for her to croak out the words, "Yeah, I'm here."

"I got your message, so I'm returning your call."

"My call?"

"Yeah, your call," Josh repeated.

"B-but I didn't call you," Cooper stammered.

"Well, I have a note here that says, 'Josh, Cooper called. Please call her.' And I'm pretty sure you're the only Cooper I know."

"But I didn't call you," Cooper insisted again.

"Okay, okay! If you say you didn't call, then you didn't call," Josh agreed.

Then it dawned on her. This must be the message she had left when she had called under the guise of needing homework help. But that was ages ago. Why was he just getting the message now?

"Wait a second, there's a date scrawled on the back of this."

"That date wouldn't happen to be from a couple weeks ago, would it?" Cooper asked.

"Yeah," Josh admitted, confusion in his voice.

"I thought so. I think I know what happened. Where'd you find that note?"

"By the phone in the kitchen."

"And that's probably where it's been since I called a while back with a question about our biology homework."

"Oh no! And I didn't call you back all this time?"

"That's okay, I'll just fail biology, have to go to summer

school, and never get into college, but it's no big deal," Cooper joked.

"Well, if that's all," Josh teased back.

Soon they were both laughing, and Cooper wondered again why they couldn't have worked things out. Their conversation was the exact opposite of the ones she'd had the night before with Micah. She and Josh could talk about anything and she never got bored. It was just like old times as he explained that band practice was keeping him busy. He told her what songs they were working on and how his guitar playing was progressing.

Cooper told him a little about Claire's parents and how difficult the last week had been. He just listened sympathetically instead of doing that boy thing of trying to find a way to fix what was wrong. After several minutes on the phone, Cooper was feeling especially brave.

"I'm meeting Claire and Alex at Cuppa Joe in a little while. Why don't you join us?" she asked, holding her breath while she waited for him to answer.

"I wish I could, but I'm meeting someone, too," Josh replied.

"Oh," Cooper said, trying to keep the disappointment out of her voice but failing miserably.

"You could always invite Micah instead," Josh suggested. The comment could have been mean except that there wasn't any malice in his tone, just a hint of a question. Cooper took the opportunity to clear things up.

"I'm not interested in Micah," Cooper said matter-of-factly.

"Then why are you dating him?"

"I'm not dating him," Cooper protested. "The only reason I agreed to go out with him is because he caught me off guard, and I couldn't think of a reason to say no that wasn't a lie."

"Oh, come on. You had a huge crush on him!"

"*Had* being the key word," Cooper pointed out. "If you want to know the truth, I would have much rather gone out with you."

"That's funny because I was working up the courage to ask you out again. But when I saw things were finally working out between you and Micah, I figured you weren't interested."

"But I was! I mean . . . I am!" Cooper practically yelled into the phone.

"I wish I had known that last week," Josh said, his voice sounding suddenly sad.

"Why?"

"Well, when I heard you and Micah make that date, it made me finally realize there was no chance of us getting back together, so I made a date, too," Josh explained.

"With who?" Cooper asked, her stomach feeling like it was trying to turn itself inside out.

"You don't know her."

"Her name wouldn't happen to be Caroline, would it?" Cooper asked, feeling sicker by the minute.

"Yeah! How'd you know that?"

"When I called and left that message, your mom thought I was her."

"Oh, that's strange. You'd like her, though. She's John Bethea's sister. I met her when we started rehearsing at their house," Josh explained, seeming not to understand at all how his words were affecting the person on the other end of the phone line.

"So just because you went out with her doesn't mean you and I can't go out again," Cooper pointed out. "I went out with Micah. We're even."

"It's not that simple."

Cooper could tell by the way he said those words that she wasn't going to like what came next.

"You know how you didn't want to lie to Micah to get out of going out with him?"

"Yeah?" Cooper hesitantly agreed, not sure where Josh was going with that.

"Well, I wanted to be just as careful not to mislead Caroline. That's why she knows all about you."

"She does?"

"Yeah. That's really how we got to know each other. She was giving me advice on you."

"And was her advice to just give up when Micah asked me out for one measly little date?" Cooper asked.

"No. By then things were more complicated. I knew Caroline sort of liked me, but I didn't want to ask her out unless I knew there was no chance of you and me working things out. So when I knew you were going out with Micah, I finally decided it didn't matter anymore so I asked her out for Friday night."

"But it was still just one date. Why can't we go out, too?"

"Because of my discipleship program."

"What discipleship program?" Cooper asked. She vaguely remembered something about Josh being discipled, but she couldn't recall where she'd heard that.

"When band practice interfered with the reading group, I signed up for this one-on-one discipleship thing through the church instead. I meet once a week with this college guy, Brian. We discuss what passages we've read that week, and then he holds me accountable on stuff."

"What kind of stuff?" Cooper wished she could stop these questions that had answers she knew she really didn't want to hear, but for some reason she couldn't.

"For one, I'm really working on following through on things, like with the band. I made a commitment to play in it for a year no matter how it goes."

"So what does that have to do with you and me?" Cooper asked, still not understanding.

"I also made a commitment to work on my relationships and to really give things a chance. I was trying to come up with a way to resolve things between us a little more when you started dating Micah."

"For the millionth time, I'm *not* dating Micah!" Cooper said, her frustration level beginning to rise.

"You know what I mean. Anyway, when I figured we were really over and saw that you were moving on—or thought you were," Josh quickly added before Cooper could protest again, "I asked Caroline out."

"You already told me that part."

"I know, but what I didn't tell you was that Brian really challenged me to not go on that first date with Caroline if I wasn't really interested, since that wouldn't be fair to her."

"And?" Cooper prodded, anxious to get to the end of this painful little story.

"And I decided I was—really interested in her, I mean. So it wouldn't be fair to go back now and tell her that just because I misunderstood your date with Micah that she and I will have to go back to just being friends while you and I start dating again."

"Well, if you explain it like that, of course it sounds unfair," Cooper protested.

"Any way you phrase it, it doesn't feel right. I can't hurt someone else so that you and I can be together," Josh explained. "What kind of a relationship would we have then?"

"I don't know," Cooper agreed, feeling guilty that she still wanted to find out. She was too emotionally drained to fight anymore, though. If this was what Josh wanted, she didn't know what else she could do.

"We can still be friends," Josh ventured.

"I know," Cooper agreed, trying not to hate those words too much.

"And you know I really do care about you."

"Me too."

"I guess I'd better let you go, then. Claire and Alex are probably waiting."

"Yeah, probably," Cooper agreed.

A moment later the phone was hung up, and Cooper couldn't help thinking she had dreamed the whole conversation.

"See, I told you he still likes you," Alex said casually, as if he were talking about a right answer on *Jeopardy* and not Cooper's life.

"Not that it does me much good," Cooper complained.

"You don't know what's going to happen in the future, though. You both still have feelings for each other, and I bet you'll be together again someday," Claire optimistically predicted. "Besides, you wouldn't want a guy who would dump someone else for you. That's just cruel."

"My head knows you're right; I just wish you could convince my heart of that."

"I know, it's hard."

"I just feel like I'm always trying so hard to do the right thing and it never turns out right. I follow my heart with Josh, and it gets stomped on. I try not to stomp on Micah's heart, and I end up having to go out with him. That ruins things with Josh. I stand up for my principles on a modeling job this week, and I get blackballed by a vindictive stylist and photographer. Tara even says I lost another job because they heard I was 'uncooperative.' And to top it all off, even our noble efforts to get your parents back together are thwarted!"

"When you put it all together like that, it does sound pretty bad," Claire agreed. "But at least where my parents are concerned, it's not a lost cause. My dad says they haven't completely ruled out marriage counseling, so I'm feeling a little hopeful."

"I'm glad someone is," Cooper said before downing the last of her double mocha.

"You know you're not ready to give up, either," Claire said. "Deep down you still believe things can turn out right."

✳   ✳   ✳

"I know you don't do the right things just to get re-warded," Cooper continued as the girls walked home after leaving Alex at the subway station. "I mean God isn't some jumbo gum ball machine where we put in the good stuff we do and get a prize in return. I just wish I knew I was on the right track. I feel like I try so hard to do what's right, but everything I do turns out wrong."

"You're exaggerating just a little, aren't you?" Claire asked gently.

"I don't know," Cooper answered. "I guess."

"Hang in there," Claire said before getting off the eleva-tor. She had her overnight bag from her stay at her dad's new place slung over one shoulder, and Cooper was convicted by her friend's good attitude. If Claire could still be hopeful in the midst of all that was going on in her life, so could she.

As the elevator rose the last three floors to her apartment, Cooper made a promise to God. "I'm going to try my best to stop looking for rewards. I know the only reward I need is that you love me and sent your Son to die for me," Cooper prayed aloud in the tight space. "Of course, I may need a reminder every now and then, but I really will try."

It wasn't much as prayers go, but Cooper knew it was a big step for her and she was smiling as she walked through the door.

"Cooper, is that you?" her mother called from down the hall.

"Yeah, I just got back from Cuppa Joe."

"There's a message for you by the phone."

Cooper experienced a brief feeling of alarm. She'd been with Claire and Alex all afternoon and she'd already talked to Josh. The only person left who could be calling was Micah! But surely after last night, he would have given up, wouldn't he?

Before she could agonize any longer, her mother put her out of her misery.

"It's from a Linda or a Lisa or something. I wrote the number down and a message."

Cooper breathed a huge sigh of relief, which was immediately replaced by curiosity. She didn't know a Linda or a Lisa. But as Cooper picked up the note by the phone and read it, she began to laugh at the irony of the situation. Hadn't she just told God it didn't matter if she saw results? Wasn't He listening in the elevator? She knew He was, though, and that was what was so funny. That she'd get a message like this now.

"God, you have a really weird sense of humor!" Cooper said aloud into the empty room once she had stopped laughing.

She looked down at the piece of paper again. On it, in her mother's neat script, were the words, *Lindsay called. She wants to cash in that favor you owe her. How about taking her to church next Sunday? Call her.*

As Cooper stared at the numbers that made up Lindsay's home phone, she found she couldn't stop smiling. Once again, this wasn't what she expected, but it was exactly what she needed at the exact right moment. True, she didn't know what the future would bring—for the Hugheses, for her and Josh, for Lindsay, for anyone—but she felt a little more at peace with the uncertainty of it all. God had proven time and time again that even in the midst of what seemed like chaos to her, He was working to bring about something good. It was a lesson she was continuously learning, and it might just slip her mind again the next time a crisis hit. But that was okay. God would be there to remind her, and that was the only certainty she really needed.

A HUNDRED MILLION KAJILLION THANKS to Melissa Riddle for knowing when to ask, when to encourage, and when to drag me out to see a movie. To my CCM friends for doing a lot of the same and for listening to me endlessly whine and pretending like I wasn't. To my family for still managing to feign interest all these books later. To Robin Jones Gunn for making it look so easy and not saying "I told you so" when I found out it wasn't. To the OHsters for always being just a mouseclick away. I don't know how I would have made it through this last year without all of you. And last but not least, to editors extraordinaire Rochelle Glöege and Cathy Engstrom, and my agent, Janet Kobobel Grant, for allowing me to push their patience to the limit while still answering my emails graciously. Your undeserved kindness to me means more than you'll ever know.